COP'S PUNISHED LITTLE

ABDL MM Romance

Jerry Hastings

ISBN: 9798446391929
Imprint: Independently published

1st edition

Cover design by: Jerry Hastings

CONTENTS

CHAPTER 1

Douglas

Thumbing away happily on the screen of my phone, I pushed the door open and entered the café. Immersed in what the screen of the phone was showing, I gave no glances in the café as I proceeded to the reception. It wasn't my first time here, so I didn't even bother looking up to the attendant. I knew who he was and also his name. A pin was glued to his uniform shirt, but I didn't even need to read it.

He waited for me until I was no more than a foot from the reception area.

"Douglas, what can I do for you today?" He asked, referencing what I should ask for breakfast this morning.

Still thumbing on the screen of my phone, I pondered that. Should I get normal, black coffee this time, just like in most of the other times I came here, or maybe get something else? How about a variation of coffee and milk? I didn't know, but I supposed it didn't matter. Whatever choice I picked, I was going to be happy with it.

Realizing that I was going to have to look at the menu, I diverted my eyes upward, finding it above Wellington's head. I skimmed it from bottom to top and then vice-versa, reading my options. Ristretto, long black, espresso, latte, and many others. I was spoiled and was aware of that.

It took me a couple of seconds, but I eventually made up my mind, "I'm going to get a cappuccino."

"Cappuccino?" He said, already grinding the coffee and operating the machines in front of him. "That's unusual for you. Did something different happen today?"

I returned my attention to the screen of the phone, thumbing on it as I responded to someone online. I was just so immersed in what I was doing that I didn't even want to look at what was around me. Not to mention that Hope River was an extremely small town and I knew that nothing around me was different from what it usually was like, anyway.

"Nothing did." I curved upward the sides of my lips.

And without saying anything else, I turned around and went to my favorite spot in the café. I sat down in it, feeling even better than normal. It was difficult to contain my excitement. I was always excited every time I came back home and could be my true self, who was utterly different from adult me.

Wellington said nothing else, still operating the machines until the cappuccino was made. I put my backpack on the floor, not even glancing at it or worrying about it. One of the advantages that came with living in such a small town was the fact that I didn't have to worry about criminals – most of the time, anyway. Sometimes, when I turned on the TV, I spotted some news reports that someone stole something in Hope River, but they were few and far between, and certainly not enough to worry me.

I could hear some people talking in the café, the door opening and closing, and a handful of cars driving in the street. It was all nothing more than background noise to me, and so I didn't pay much attention to them.

I was still typing on my phone, writing a long text wall about something that people should be more concerned about, and that was the dangerous environmental changes that we were inflicting on the planet. Why were they so blind? They even wanted to build a shopping mall in the downtown region and I couldn't wrap my head around that. Why were people so willing to accept that when it was going to change everything here fundamentally? I didn't know, but I was a fighter and wasn't going to drop the issue. I was going to do everything in my power to bring as much change as possible.

I clicked on the send button when I finally exhaled and felt that I could relax a little. It took me a long while to prepare that text and I knew that my followers were going to love it. Nevertheless, what I wanted the most right now was to reach new readers.

I put my phone on the table as I glanced up, finding something else on it. The first thought that popped up in my mind was what that even was. It took me a second to realize that the shape was exactly like that of a book, but also slightly different.

It was a book and nothing more than that. I shook my head, smiling gently as I realized that I was so immersed in my virtual world that it took me a while to figure out that that was nothing more than a book.

It wasn't open, but something about it was piquing my interest, and that was the fact that nothing was written on the cover. I perked up my left eyebrow, wondering what that meant. Either the book was extremely old to the point that whatever was once written on the cover faded away a long time ago, or it was a draft for a new story.

I glanced from side to side, wondering if the owner of the book was anywhere nearby. I spotted some people around me, but none that could be coming this way. *Curiosity killed the cat* was the first thing that popped up in my mind when I reached for the book, ignoring that saying. It wasn't going to deter me from satisfying my curiosity.

I picked up the book quickly and opened it, noticing right away that it was handwritten. This time, I perked up both of my eyebrows. I didn't think I was going to find a book on the table where I usually sat and much less that it was handwritten. The writing wasn't beautiful to look at, but it was clear enough and I could make out the words.

I was just reading it when, out of the blue, I noticed a shadow emerging and darkening the space where I was seated. My body froze up, but I still slowly turned my head to the side, noticing the cream uniform, then his waistline, the chest, and then his beard.

His eyes were glaring at me, and they were coconut-colored eyes. His hair was cut short, the tone the same color as his eyes. Given the texture of his face, I could tell that he was most likely in his mid-30s, which was a positive for him, not that I thought he was even thinking about that, though.

Given how tense his jawline looked, I could tell that he wasn't pleased by what he was seeing.

"Is this book yours?" I asked, moving my hands to the left so that he noticed that I was going to give the book to him.

"Yes," he replied, his voice deep and throaty. It was almost like he was doing everything in his power not to hurt me right now, even though I could tell that, deep in his heart, he wasn't someone that could even hurt a fly. I could feel care coming out of him, which was something that, at first glance, most people wouldn't even think possible.

He snatched the book out of my hand and I said, "I'm sorry, officer. I didn't mean to pry."

"Obviously not," he said and I turned my eyes to the right, finding his nameplate. Officer Roderick Castillo... It was a beautiful name and I was going to keep it in mind. I should know who this person was, given how small Hope River was, and yet I didn't. It was the first time that we were meeting in person. Why that was like this, I had no idea. It was possible, but unlikely that maybe... he was new?

After a couple of seconds, I asked, "Are you writing it? What is it about?"

He tensed up his jaw again and I almost flinched. I thought that he was going to hit me, which was silly. After all, it was unlikely that he was going to hurt me in a place where everyone could see it.

"My life..." He responded and then a crack of a noise coming from the little device hanging from the side of his chest caught his attention. A voice came from it moments later, asking Roderick what he was doing right now. And then, he said after they had a short conversation, "I'm going there in a bit."

He gave me one last glance before turning around and leaving with his book. I let out a sigh of relief as I realized that things could have turned out much worse if his partner hadn't called him to do whatever it was that they were going to do. I relaxed my body in the seat and turned my eyes to the left again when I noticed Wellington putting my order on the table.

"Bon appetit," he said with half a smile on his face before turning and leaving until he was behind the front desk again.

I was left looking at the cup of cappuccino and wondering what just happened. Who was Roderick and why was he so pissed at me?

CHAPTER 2

Roderick

Did nobody in this town know the concept of privacy? I asked myself, turning my head left and right as I then drove the car through the next intersection, just cruising across the town. My partner had called me about a developing situation in one of the most troublesome neighborhoods in Hope River, but it turned out to be a bust. When we got there, ready to imprison a criminal, which was something that hadn't happened here in months, we found out that the culprit was just a big dog that jumped through a window, breaking into the house.

We got him out of there and took him to the owner, and that was that. Not much else happened since then, which was a fact highlighted by how often I was yawning right now. My hands were on the steering wheel and I was driving the vehicle, but I was barely paying attention to the road and to what was happening around me.

One of the big reasons behind that was that my mind kept going back to that guy who tried reading what I was writing. I had no idea what was even going on in my mind when I left my book on that table unattended. It was always so important to me, containing information on my life that nobody should know about. If they did, I wouldn't be sure that I would still be on the force.

And one of the things that glued my mind to that young man was how cute and beautiful he looked. He was truly out-of-this-world good-looking, which was certainly something that wasn't a constant in this town.

And yes, that meant that I was gay, which was one of the biggest reasons why everything that was in the book needed to be kept hidden behind several locked doors. I was going to be a lot more dutiful regarding where I kept or left my book from now on, I promised myself.

I pulled over to a parking space close to the place where they were going to build a huge shopping mall. I could see some workers working on the construction, lifting heavy blocks with their machines. From where I was, I could barely hear the noise that they were making. Some of the neighbors didn't like it at all, but there was nothing that they could do about it. The owners of the shopping mall that was going to be built had money that the town needed and we needed to make sure that they still thought that the town was a good place for them to keep investing here.

It was a shitshow. So much so that I didn't even want to be remembering that right now.

I picked up my book again and opened it when I noticed that someone was driving in the parking space. I noticed the car swerving and finishing maneuvers that I deemed too dangerous, even for someone skilled. Either that, or whoever was driving it didn't know what they were doing, and if that was the case, I needed to interfere.

When I was going to do that, the car was parked when my hand was already turning the ignition key.

Huh, how weird, I thought to myself, examining what the guy behind the steering wheel was going to do next. In the following minutes, nothing happened and I was much more relieved. If that person had little to no knowledge about driving, then I hoped he had someone teaching them.

I closed my eyes as I realized that most likely nothing else was going to happen right now. Everything around me was quiet, excluding some noises of cars driving on the road and the workers constructing the shopping mall. The sun was bright and cheerful, making everything around me a little warm, but not too much so. It was at about the right temperature.

But then, the sound of something metallic crashing made me jump in my seat, throwing my eyes open at the same moment. I peered outside the windshield as I noticed two cars crashed against each other, and one of them was the same one that I had spotted in the parking space before. A stream of smoke was going up from the engine, signaling that I had to go there right away.

Noticing that, I turned on the engine and then the siren of my police car, thrusting my right foot onto the accelerator pedal. The car lunged forward, rushing over there as fast as the engine could take it. As I hurried over to where the accident happened, I called for backup just in case something I didn't expect happened. It was most likely unnecessary, but that was okay.

I pulled over where the accident took place, opening the car's door as I stepped out. I thought I was going to find nothing more than a car accident where both parties were going to come out of it unscathed, but what happened was much more serious than that. The car closest to me crashed into the other one hard, the front smashed and utterly destroyed. My gut twisted in a knot as I peered inside the vehicle and noticed that the driver that was in it was none other than the same guy that I had run into at the café.

His body was pressed up against the front of the vehicle, his head lolled to the side. Blood was coming out of his nose and ears, and his eyes were closed. I felt a knot in my stomach as I thought that he had to be dead. I didn't want to think that he was, but I didn't think that someone who suffered such a heavy accident could actually pull through. His arms were splayed out over the console and his fingers weren't even moving.

As if this was some kind of joke, everything around me was still cheerful and pristine. Tree canopies swayed gently in the wind and everyone at the construction site was still doing their duty, noises of machinery and shouts coming from there.

I reached out and opened the door, trying to pull him out of there as gently as I could. The frame and the vehicle itself were almost trying to become one with him, thrust against his body. His stomach's skin was dilacerated and blood was coming out of the holes. After I pulled him out of there, his body fell gently on the road. I put him on the side of his vehicle and then reached out for the device strapped to my uniform and pressed a button.

A voice came from the other side of the call and I asked for an ambulance. They said that they were going to come here as soon as possible, but after I ended the call, I was already impatient. Tapping my foot on the ground, I was already looking left and right as I wondered how many more minutes it was going to take them to get here. They couldn't take much longer, or else this guy, who pissed me off so much when I caught him reading my book without permission, wasn't going to pull through. And if that happened, it would ruin my month.

Regardless, this wasn't about me, but him. As a police officer, all I wanted was to see him well.

As if to show me that I shouldn't be so worried, he cracked open his eyes slowly and looked up. The rest of his body wasn't moving, but he was awake – or just barely so.

I dropped to one knee right away, grabbing his hand and feeling how cold it was. I brushed my hand over it slowly as I tried to show him that everything was going to be okay and that I had this situation over control, even though that wasn't precisely the case.

"I just called the ambulance. They're going to come and make you feel better right away. You don't need to worry."

"You are that guy…" He said and then his eyes closed again, making my heart somersault in my chest. I hoped that those weren't his last words, but anything was possible at the moment. All I knew was that the ambulance had to get here as soon as possible.

As if it was reading my mind, I heard the siren sounding in the distance and nearing where we were. I let out a sigh of relief when it turned at the intersection and then pulled over harshly.

I put my arms around him and pulled him up, ready to take

him to the ambulance. No matter what happened, he was going to get the best treatment possible, I promised.

CHAPTER 3

Douglas

When I reopened my eyes, he was seated by my side, his hands clasped in his lap. His head was tilted down and his eyes were half-closed. He was the same police officer from before, who seemed so angry when he caught me reading his book without permission. He was the one that saved me, wasn't he?

I turned my eyes left and right slowly, realizing that I couldn't feel the rest of my body. I couldn't move my fingers, my arms, or my legs. I was on a hospital bed, my body covered with a white blanket. It was thin and light, almost like it wasn't there. I could hear a machine by my side beeping slowly. It was a heart monitoring machine and it showed me that at least my heart was okay.

Nevertheless, that wasn't enough to quench my fears. I couldn't move my body and I barely had enough strength to say anything. The police officer was still with his head lowered and I had no idea what was going on in his mind. I did have some friends here in Hope River, but I didn't have my family here and thus it made sense that I was alone, not counting him.

My head was all bandaged up, which made me more worried that something truly terrible happened. I was training my driving in that parking space when I decided to venture onto the road and tackle what real driving was like. I was quite ashamed of myself that I was already 19 and didn't know how to drive properly yet.

I had a cheap, run-of-the-mill car that was enough for me, but I first needed my driver's license so that I could drive around with it comfortably.

When I ventured onto the road, I was so certain that I could finally drive on some stretches of the road without panicking, but it appeared that that had been nothing more than an illusion. I said that because the accident had to have happened as a result of my reckless choice. My friends had to have come here to see me when I was still unconscious. That's what made sense to me, even though I was still curious about what the police officer had to say to me. He had to have been involved in the accident somehow, and I didn't think that he was the one that put me on this hospital bed.

I tried to move my finger, but it was impossible and it netted me no result. As I tried to utter something, Roderick finally looked up, noticing that I was already awake. I thought that I was going to see the same face of that man that instilled fear in me, but I perceived something else. He opened a smile, which wasn't big and bright, but still showed that he was happy that he was seeing that I was already awake.

He even stood up slowly, taking two steps toward me. It was as if he didn't know what to do with his hands, which was certainly news to me. A police officer of his caliber certainly knew how to deal with any situation, including this one. He looked impeccable, clean, and the fragrance coming from him was intoxicating, and it filled my lungs.

The man was a beefcake and my type. Even while I was still so worried about my health, that was the first – or I should say, one of the first – thoughts that popped up in my mind now that I was awake.

"Douglas… I'm sorry. I didn't ask your name when we first met at the café, but I'm just so happy that you are awake."

"What happened? I don't understand. I can't move my body."

He lowered his eyebrows, his face assuming a sadder tone.

"You were in an accident. Your car crashed into another and

you were badly hurt. I should have been paying more attention to what was happening around me. It was my fault," he lamented, pulling the chair so that he was sitting closer to me.

"And why can't I move my body?" I asked and the question hung in the air like something that shouldn't have been brought up. Roderick diverted his eyes downward, avoiding my stare. That was a bad sign and I didn't like it. If anything, it just made me more worried about everything.

"You broke your spine in the accident and I'm afraid you can't walk anymore-"

And just as he finished saying that, it was like my heart was just pierced by a lance. The world started to spin around me, making me feel dizzy, or maybe that was just my mind thinking that that was happening. Regardless, my eyes closed halfway and I felt my body losing its strength. It was already weak, to begin with, but now it was like it didn't even exist anymore. I waited until I could feel that I could move my legs and arms again, but that never happened and nothing changed since he expressed those words.

Noticing my reaction, he grabbed my hand and I couldn't feel it. I couldn't feel his hand on me, making my heart speed up. I panicked again and suddenly found myself dreaming that this was nothing more than a nightmare. If I couldn't even feel his hand on mine, then whatever hope I had left that I could still walk again and be the bubbly guy I used to be was lost. He said that I broke my spine and I didn't even have enough money to pay for any available treatment, if there was any.

"Douglas, hey, stay with me!" He raised his voice, piercing through my stupor. Roderick brought me right back into the real world, which was painful and not what I wanted right now. It was as if my old self was part of a life that I was never going to have again, which I was pretty sure was the case.

I wasn't even going to be able to diaper myself, which hurt me more deeply than anything else. I loved being a little and now that was part of my past.

Snapping my eyes open, I said, "But why should I continue living in this world when I can't even do the things that I want to?"

He squeezed my hand tightly and I could feel just the tiny little hint that he was grabbing it, but it wasn't enough. If there was hope that I could move my body freely like before, that wasn't sufficient. The truth was that my old self was over and dead.

"There is much more to life than that," he said, sitting back down on his chair when he realized that I already felt less panicked. But he didn't retreat his hand like I was afraid he was going to, which was a plus. He kept on holding my hand even though I couldn't feel it. I couldn't feel anything other than what my head and neck could. My case was severe and that was something that was already so deeply ingrained in my mind that it didn't matter what the doctors told me – they weren't going to make me believe that I could become like my old self again.

I turned my head to the left slowly, looking outside and hearing some kids playing there. They were happy, hopping and running around without a care in the world. I wanted to be like them, I wanted to be able to work out, play, and run around without a worry in the world, but that was impossible now.

I felt a tear coming out and I didn't do anything to contain it. I didn't have any hopes that things were going to get better and I could already feel depression creeping in. I contemplated it, but I didn't welcome it – not yet, anyway.

Minutes later, when Roderick thought that I had already calmed down, he finally pulled back his hand, even though it was like he was still holding mine.

"The doctors said that you don't live with anyone here. Do you have a friend or anyone that can take care of you?" He asked.

I lowered my head, thinking that there was no point in lying to Roderick. Not to mention that if I did something like that, it would only make things worse, anyway.

I shook my head and responded, "No, I don't think there is. I live by myself here."

"Then, I'm going to look after you."

I snapped my head at him. "What?" I asked, sounding flabbergasted. I couldn't have sounded any different even if I wanted to. The last thing I thought that could happen after the accident was him offering to look after me.

And it appeared that I couldn't change his mind.

CHAPTER 4

Roderick

Offering my help was the sensible thing to do right now and he accepted it, which was a plus. It was much more than that, actually. Even if Douglas had said no, I would still have insisted on the subject. In the beginning, he was surprised at my proposal, but then he was more receptive to it when he realized that he didn't have another option. He couldn't move, was in a wheelchair, and needed someone to do things that he would otherwise do alone.

After I pulled over, I opened the door and grabbed him. I helped him sit in his wheelchair, adjusted him so that he was sitting comfortably on it, and then closed the door of the police car. I looked around me, noticing that the neighborhood where he lived was high-end and friendly. I could see children playing in front of their homes, running around and shouting words that I couldn't make out.

The sky was cyan blue, the sun was bright and beautiful, and I could also see some butterflies flying around the trees.

In other circumstances, Douglas would be with a big, happy smile on his face as he hopped around with his phone and had a lot of fun texting with his friends, but today was different. Today was the first day when the hospital gave him the green light and he was allowed back to his home.

After some paperwork, the local government told me that I could look after him for as long as needed. Given that I didn't have a family and that I also didn't have to look after anyone else, I was the perfect fit. Not to mention that the town was pretty small and I could come back here, every time it was needed, in a heartbeat. And in addition to that, my hours were also lowered so that I could spend more time with Douglas. There were a lot of things that he was going to need help with, including taking baths and eating. It wasn't going to be easy, but I was sure that he could pull through.

In the meantime, he could cling to the hope that the doctors said he might be able to regain what he lost. He might be able to move his body freely again. He could still feel little tingles on his skin when someone touched him, like I did when he woke up from his coma, but it wasn't certain that he would eventually be able to become his old self. I said that because what he was going through was going to leave a deep scar on him.

I grabbed the handles of the wheelchair, turning it so that he was looking at his home.

I didn't have to look at his face to know that he didn't seem pleased by what he was seeing.

"I'm going to feel like a prisoner in there," he grumbled, wishing that he could fold his arms over his chest so that he could make his point clearer. Douglas still looked so pretty and cute in the wheelchair, especially with his pair of glasses on, but the lack of happiness on his face was telling and it pierced my heart. I wanted nothing more than to bring his smile back to his face, but I knew I couldn't do that right now.

"I'm going to be here with you anytime you need."

"And in the meantime, when you aren't there, I'm going to be a prisoner and pretty much useless."

"You'll still be able to study. It's going to be different, but you will be able to learn everything you want."

"But I won't be able to perform my job when I graduate. I'll be useless. I'll always need someone to look after me."

"Your friends can also come here to help you," I said, guiding the wheelchair toward the porch of his house. It was a common, white, and middle-class-looking home. It even had a garage, though his car wasn't in there. It was in the scrapyard and that was where it was going to remain for the time being until someone bought what was left of it.

"My friends are nice and I care about them, but when they realize that I need too much of their help, they'll leave me alone. They'll abandon me."

"If they really are your friends, then that won't happen."

After some seconds, he said, "You sound so happy because you can still walk and do everything freely and the way you are used to. That's not the case for me anymore. I can't feel happy about life any longer."

I sighed, shaking my head. It was going to take a while to convince Douglas that he could live a happy and normal life again. Maybe even months or years, but I was pretty sure I could make that happen.

We were halfway to the porch of his house when I said, "It's nothing like that. I'm just trying to cheer you up so that you feel better. The doctors said that you feeling better is important so that you get better too. You're going to have your therapy sessions and everything else you need until you can walk again."

"I don't have enough money for those things," he grumbled again, lowering his head in shame. His parents paid for his college, but they didn't have enough money to pay for his treatment. That was where I came in, which was something I thought I would never do for someone else after the disappointment I had with my previous partner. He shattered my heart and I could never forgive him for that.

"I'm going to pay for everything that your family can't cover," I announced and he turned his head so that he could look at me from the corner of his vision.

"What? You can't be serious about that. You'll go bankrupt."

"I have some money saved up and I don't need it."

And I did, a little. When my father passed away, he left a lot of money for me. I kept it all in my savings account and only used it when absolutely necessary. Now was one of those moments, I thought. I couldn't see myself spending that money on something else. Douglas needed it for his treatment and he was going to get it.

Douglas was still with his head turned and looking at me from the corner of his eye.

"You can't be serious. You must be joking. You're just a police officer. You can't have all that money available. You're going to need tens of thousands, if not more than that, to pay for the treatment."

"You're underestimating me. I have enough money for the treatment and I won't go bankrupt. You can rest assured about that," I affirmed, pulling the wheelchair over the porch steps and landing it gently on the porch itself. We went to the door, I had the key, and then I opened it.

"You gotta be joking. Not to mention that I already feel terrible that you have to look after me." And after a moment of silence, when we were still on the porch and I waited until he finished, he added, "You are a good man. I'm so sorry that I opened your book without permission."

"Hey, it's nothing. It's just something very personal to me and even though you were crossing a line that you shouldn't have, I'm not going to hold it against you."

"Phew, that's a relief," he said when we walked through the doorway and I stopped the wheelchair in front of the huge TV. "Still, I can't feel good knowing that you're spending so much money because of me. It isn't right."

"As I said, it's nothing."

I didn't ask Douglas if he wanted me to turn on the TV. I just turned it on and left it on a TV series. It appeared to be a zombie-themed TV show, which should be to Douglas' taste, right? And yet, I felt that that wasn't the case.

I walked around the wheelchair, finding myself in front of Douglas. He was watching the screen, but the lack of a smile on his face was telling. He wasn't content with what the channel was playing right now.

The remote was still in my hand. I pressed the button to change to the next channel, which showed a colorful and happy cartoon. He curled up the sides of his lips slightly and seemed more content now. Seeing his reaction, I left the remote on the couch. Since he couldn't even move his hands, he couldn't change the channel, which made me realize more strongly how much he was going to need me right now.

The question was – could he look past that and find joy in his new life? I didn't know, but I knew that he was going to need me if he was going to have a chance at that.

CHAPTER 5

Having Roderick around was great, even better than being alone the way I was before. I had friends – plenty of them, in fact – but they were never around when I truly needed them, just like now. It wasn't that they avoided coming here, but given that they had their classes and that my classes were online, they couldn't come here as often as they would like. Still, they were beginning to visit me more frequently these last few days.

I was still trying to cope with the fact that my body, from my neck down, was paralyzed. I could feel depression creeping in and I knew that it was eventually going to overtake my once overly happy mind, but for now, Roderick was holding all the pieces that composed me together. He was always here, even when he couldn't and was supposed to be working.

I had plenty of items for littles in my house, which prompted him to ask me several questions about them. I couldn't tell him that I was a little and I never would. Roderick could have insisted a little more on the subject when he noticed my diapers in the closet, but he dropped his questions before I ran out of half-assed answers. I imagined that he didn't want to put more pressure on me than I already had.

Roderick was always respectful, always looking after me. I just hated the fact that I was finally spending time with someone I could imagine becoming my daddy and living the rest of my life with him, and that this was all happening because I was useless. My body served no purpose anymore, I couldn't move my fingers, and I hated myself.

The smell that came from the kitchen was delicious, wafting in the air. I didn't know what he was making, but it was likely going to feel weird – and also, right - when he was putting the spoon with the food in my mouth, feeding me. I never thought that one day I would find myself in this situation, paraplegic. I just felt so useless.

On my lap was my little, super cute teddy bear and I couldn't even hold him with my fingers. It was one of the things that most hurt my heart right now.

It was dark outside, the moon above the buildings and the moonlight shining through the window. It was supposed to feel homey, but it didn't feel that way at all. I still felt like I was a prisoner in my own house. It didn't help things that my caretaker was a police officer, I thought amusingly.

I could hear him humming in the kitchen as he leaped from stove to fridge and then to the counters, where he prepared the food. He asked me several questions about what kind of food I liked and I answered all of them. I was pretty sure that he was making something that I was going to love, which made me real-ize that now things were happening exactly the way I always wanted.

I had a caretaker, someone to look after me every day, who even helped me when I had to use the bathroom. He bathed me, helped me sit on the toilet when I needed to, and wiped my butt. I never thought I would find someone mature enough to do those things for me without it feeling weird. I mean, it was pretty weird in the beginning when I was getting used to it, but now I was more accustomed to it.

I was in my wheelchair, watching TV. My favorite cartoon was being played on the channel, which was pretty much one of the few things I could still enjoy about my life. Another was the fact that I didn't have to worry about anything that didn't involve me getting better. I couldn't even get angry at anything. My mind was numbed, neutered. It was perfect that way. I wasn't supposed to get angry, anyway.

Moments later, when the cartoon reached a point in it that I didn't like at all, Roderick swooped in through the doorway, holding a plate in his hands. I could barely see it from the corner of my eyes, loving the smell that was only getting stronger.

I could make out the chicken, the rice, and other foods that composed the meal. My stomach rumbled when I noticed that he made a combination of every food that I liked. I didn't even know what that meal should be called, but it felt and looked delicious. The steam lines going up from the plate told me as much.

"I hope you like it. I decided to make something different," he said, pulling over a chair so that he could sit on it and was right in front of me. I had a highchair, which… he could potentially use so that he could put the plate on it and feed me more easily that way.

As a little, I couldn't help but wonder if it was possible to do this differently. What if he could put me in the highchair and feed me while I was seated in it? I didn't know, but the question nagged my mind and I didn't know if I could keep ignoring it.

Roderick must've noticed the struggle on my face because, suddenly, he asked, "Is there something else you want? Something I missed?"

He was always like that, always looking after me and trying to read what I was thinking. Now that I was thinking about it, it hurt me so much the way we first met. I was snooping through his stuff. I should never have done that, regardless of how curious I was.

"No, it's nothing. Don't worry about what I'm thinking right now."

He settled his hand on mine, looking deeply into my eyes with love and care. I didn't know if his love meant more than what I thought it did, but I hoped it did. This whole time, now that he was already living with me for a couple of weeks, I hadn't yet asked him anything about his family. I knew that he lived alone here as well, but I didn't know anything about his past and what happened in it. We were so busy with my recovery that we didn't even bother broaching those topics.

"Worrying about you is everything that I do nowadays," he said, his voice gentler. I took a deep breath in and studied his eyes. I could tell that Roderick wasn't going to drop it. He wanted to know everything that was going on in my mind and I had no choice but to answer him.

"I feel ashamed of it. I don't think I should even mention what it is."

He brushed his hand over mine, caressing it. It was almost like we were lovers, except that we weren't. There was no way we could even become more than what we were, which was friends.

I exhaled and looked down when I responded, "Could you put me in the highchair? You noticed that it's big enough for me. I know that I'm not a big person, to begin with, but I fit perfectly in the highchair."

He looked at the highchair with some confusion in his eyes, almost like he wondered what was the true story behind my acquisition. When he realized that it was better not to bring that up, he said, "Sure thing. Why not? If it makes you feel better and especially if it brings your smile back, then it's worth it."

He put the plate on the couch, 'opened' the highchair, and put me in it. Then, he 'closed' the highchair and put the plate on the support in front of me. The first few seconds were a little weird, but also extremely exciting. I wanted to dig in, to gobble up all the food that he made for me, but I couldn't. I tried moving my fingers again, but I couldn't even feel them. I then pushed that thought out of my mind and decided not to focus on it.

And as he fed me with the spoon, a little piece of the food that I was eating fell out of my mouth and landed on my shirt.

When he noticed that, Roderick said, "Oh, look at the mess you just made. I'm going to have to change that about you." And the way that he said that could have been perfect if he had bumped up the pitch of his voice, making it sound more child-like, as if he was talking to a kid.

I was dreaming things that could never happen, I thought. There was no way that he would ever do something like that with me. He was an adult, knew that I was also an adult, and was also aware that it would be weird if he raised the pitch of his voice like that.

All I knew was that I was loving that he was feeding me. It was just like he was my Daddy and I was his little. And to make things even more fitting, I had a special request to make for him.

CHAPTER 6

Roderick

I had to admit that looking after Douglas was tough work. He needed me all the time and that coupled with the fact that I still had to work as a police officer made things even more complicated, but I was managing. I had more than enough money to cover our expenses, which were plentiful. They were taking a hit on my bank account, which was something I never thought would happen. Before I had to look after Douglas, the number that composed the summary of my savings account was only going up. After all, I spent less money than what I made as a police officer.

Douglas couldn't help but feel that he was to blame for that. I tried to show him that he was wrong about that, but if there was something that I learned about him, it was that he was always stubborn. When he wanted something, he wasn't just overly curious, but also so stubborn that he could hurt himself.

I was just happy that things appeared to be progressing relatively well these last weeks. The therapies were working, though his progress wasn't something visual yet. There was this one moment when we thought he moved his finger, but it actually didn't happen.

When I entered his house, I was curious about the items that I saw spread around not just in the living room, but also all over. I had no idea what was going on when I spotted a small teddy bear on his bed and a big pony that he could ride in his bedroom, but it piqued my interest and I started to look into it. I didn't delve too far into it because I didn't want to feel like I was doing something behind his back.

Nevertheless, it was weird when I found out that he had a highchair in his kitchen. I tried to ask him questions about that, but he always changed the subject to something that he was more comfortable with.

"Roderick, if you don't mind, there's something that I would like you to do for me," he mentioned, making me stop the spoon mid-air. I was going to give him another spoonful of mashed potatoes and some other things that I whipped up for him, but the way he said that made me stop.

Raising my right eyebrow, I asked, "What is it?"

"I have some bibs in one of the cupboards. It's right over there," he said, turning his head to the right. I knew which cupboard he was talking about. It was the only one that, during the entire time that I had been looking after him, I hadn't opened yet. "Could you put one on my neck? I don't want to dirt my shirt again while eating."

I blinked twice, finding it unbelievable that he also had bibs in his collection on top of everything else he already had.

"Sure thing," I still said, putting the spoon on the highchair's tray and going to the cupboard. I opened it and, after some searching, I found what I was looking for. He had an extensive collection of bibs, and they all looked childish and cheerful. They were quite cute, if I could say without sounding weird.

I still had so many questions to ask Douglas about all these childish things that he had in his house. He didn't look like the kind of person that was once a father, I reaffirmed.

After thinking that, I grabbed the boxes where the bibs were and finished opening it. I picked up one of the bibs and went back to him. I stood behind Douglas and looped the bib around his neck. When it was hanging from it, I almost wanted to snap a picture of him, but I knew that it would be weird. It was for that reason that

I didn't even say anything about that.

I went back to being in front of him, filling another spoon with his dinner. He opened his mouth wide and, this time, he actually looked happy, which was something that I thought was going to take a while until I witnessed it again.

He munched what was in his mouth, swallowing it moments after.

"You should chew more before swallowing," I advised, sounding like a true father worried about his kid, which was something I thought would never happen in my life, me being gay and all.

He widened his smile, saying, "I'm going to be more careful, from now on. How could it be any different when I have someone like you looking after me?"

"Good point, Douglas," I said and finished feeding him what was on the plate. When it was over, I was almost sad. I thought that the dinner was going to be stretched out for a lot longer, lasting longer than the 30 minutes where I shared a good moment with him.

"Ohhhh, I'm sad that it's already over," he said, wishing that he could be doing a lot more now, but also reminding himself that he couldn't because he was paraplegic.

Seeing that, I couldn't help but let sadness flow into my heart. As long as he finished his therapies properly, everything was going to be fine, I reaffirmed.

"There's dinner and lunch tomorrow as well," I said, and that appeared to cheer him up.

After dinner, I did the dishes, dried my hands, and then came back to the living room, where I found Douglas with his head resting on his shoulder. He was sleeping and I just caught him napping again.

I took the bib off his neck, threw it into the hamper where it was going to be until the weekend, and then picked him up in my arms. I turned off the light in the living room and also the TV, proceeding to the stairs that took me to the second floor of his house.

It was a big house, especially for someone living alone before I showed up in his life. I thought that I could manage to live in my house and take care of him, but I wasn't able to. I was saving a lot more time by living here in his house than I did while I was still living in my old one, I remembered.

I opened the door of his bedroom and went to his bed. I pulled up the comforter and tucked him under it, thinking that he should probably take a bath tonight, but deciding that it was probably better that he didn't. I just didn't want to wake him up, I thought to myself.

I stayed maybe a couple of seconds just admiring Douglas while he slept before I realized that what I was doing was probably creepy, especially because I was nothing more than his friend, even though I had a crush on him.

"Sleep well, Douglas," I whispered to myself, reminding myself that one of the things that he most liked was the little teddy bear that he always had with him. Thinking that, I went to the living room again, where I found it on the couch. I picked it up in my right hand and hopped back to his bedroom, wondering if maybe he moved during his sleep, but that was probably just my imagination playing tricks on me.

I grabbed his arm and lifted it gently, tucking the little teddy bear underneath it. Douglas stirred softly, but didn't open his eyes. His breathing remained controlled, which reassured me that he was really still sleeping.

I stayed maybe a couple seconds watching him to make sure that he wasn't pretending that he was sleeping and then I went back to the door, even though I didn't want to. I slept in the room where he had a piano and a couple of other things, including canvases, where he could practice art.

Even though he was extremely extroverted most of the time, and especially before the accident, he could be quite introspective when he wanted. He liked playing the piano and painting, which were things that I just couldn't imagine myself doing. I was a little rougher when it came to my cultural side, I thought with some sadness in my heart.

Even if Douglas was gay, we couldn't really connect. The age gap between us was quite significant and he liked things that I didn't like, I also thought.

A relationship between us was never going to happen.

CHAPTER 7

I woke up the next morning, streaks of light coming through the window. The sun was shining brightly in the morning and there was a light rain falling outside. It was one of those calming, everlasting rains that just refused to stop. I wanted to be out there, playing in it, but I couldn't. I should be happy that I could at least turn my neck, even though that was a far cry from what I could do when I was my normal self.

My normal self... Somehow, it was like that happened eons ago.

If there was one thing that I wanted to do this morning, it was slipping back into my little self. I wanted to be a little, to act like one, to pretend that I was a baby and that I couldn't even talk, that everything that came out of my mouth was nothing more than incomprehensible gibberish. I would baby talk, have a pacifier in my mouth, and play with my little teddy bear like it was the most important thing in the world to me, even though that wasn't true at the moment. The most important thing wasn't even a 'thing' anymore - it was a person. The same one that was looking after me, always making sure that I was fed and well-rested.

The door opened moments later, when I was already sullen and brooding. I was looking down, staring at my legs and wondering if it was possible, that they could move again if I applied enough effort into that. I was pretty sure that the doctors were full of shit, but maybe that wasn't true. Different doctors already told me that there was a slight chance I could recover from being paraplegic.

The person that opened the door was, of course, none other than Roderick. He wasn't even working anymore – at least not as often as before – as a police officer. It was good having more time with him, but it also made me feel a little bad. It was like I was a parasite that was taking more and more of his time. I knew that he didn't look at it that way, but I still couldn't help but think things differently.

"Morning, sleepyhead. Did you sleep well?" He asked, stepping toward me and stopping by the side of the bed.

"Yes, I did," I responded, feeling even more connected to Roderick than I did before. He was always so caring and loving, which were perfect attributes to be a Daddy, even though I knew he could never be.

"C'mon, let me get you off the bed and into the bathroom. You didn't take a bath last night and we need to rectify that."

He pulled off my comforter and was going to loop his arms around me when I said, "Roderick, do you mind if I ask you something?"

He stopped his arms, letting them fall to the sides of his body. He regarded me with curiosity as he lifted his left eyebrow.

"Sure, whatever you want to ask me," he replied and I knew that I had the green light to ask my question.

I cleared my throat as I prepared myself for it. This whole time, living with Roderick all these weeks, and it was only until now that I mustered up enough courage to ask him that question.

"Roderick… Do you have a family? Do you have a partner or someone that you are interested in?"

He widened his eyes slightly, but then they quickly went back to normal. A chair was by his side and he sat on it slowly, letting all the air that was in his lungs come out.

"I figured that this question was going to pop up eventually."

I gave him some time as he pondered his words. Then, he continued, "I have family, but they live in New York. Right now, in this town, all I have is you and my friends from the force."

"And… Is there someone that you want as your partner?"

He peered into my eyes gently, almost as if he was showing me he was suspicious of something.

"Why do you want to know that?" He asked and I had no idea if I was crossing a line I shouldn't. I was just curious, maybe overly so again.

"I want to get to know you better. We've been living together for a while, but I still don't know much about your family or what you do when you aren't here."

He turned his head to look outside the window before he said, "There is someone, but I don't think that he wants me."

I widened my eyes at the same moment. I couldn't believe he just said that. "You mean that he is… a guy?" I asked. My voice was throaty and weak. His words caught me off guard.

"Yeah, he is."

"I didn't think you were-"

"Gay?" He asked, turning his head so that his eyes were looking at me again. "Whenever someone finds that out about me, they're always surprised. To be honest, I always keep it hidden unless it gets brought up, just like now. I feel like I can trust you with that information."

I opened and closed my mouth like I was a goldfish. I looked so stupid and there was nothing that could be done about that. "You don't need to worry. I'll never tell anyone that."

He curled up the left side of his lips. "Thanks. As I said, I knew I could trust you."

After a moment of silence, as I pondered my next words, I then finally said, "There is also something you need to know about me."

He perked up his left eyebrow. "Really? Then, tell me if you feel comfortable with that."

I cleared my throat before continuing, "I also like… guys."

He widened his eyes slightly and, for a moment, we both didn't say anything. He was equally shocked that he now knew that I was gay. We both thought that we were straight, just like most men in town.

"Have you ever dated?" He asked.

I shook my head.

"So, you are a virgin?"

I nodded. I felt heat rising to my cheeks, but there was nothing that could be done about it. I felt uncomfortable talking about that part of my life and I couldn't stop what was happening. Now that Roderick knew that I was gay, he was going to want to know everything about me.

"Is there a reason why you haven't yet?"

I looked down, pursing my lips. I just realized that even if there was someone I wanted, other than Roderick, it wouldn't really matter. As a paraplegic, I wouldn't be able to give him what he wanted. That was a given and it was something that was forever going to be ingrained in my mind.

"It's just this town. It's always bringing me down, always reminding me that I live surrounded by conservatives, and that they are ready to bring out their pitchforks if they find out about that part of my life. They already think that I look and act too feminine."

He curled up the side of his lips and grabbed my hand, brushing his thumb over the back of it. I hated that I couldn't feel his finger doing that. My body was just so useless and it was decaying over time. Since I couldn't exercise my muscles, they were becoming thinner and lighter.

"This is a nice town, but I know what you're saying. Sometimes, it can be too tiresome, especially when you can't be who you are. I've certainly been in a similar situation many times before. I suppose I should be saying that I was lucky because I lived elsewhere before coming here, though."

"That's really lucky..." I said, murmuring to myself as I

lowered my head.

It was nice that we were bonding even more strongly than before, but everything that I learned about him wasn't sufficient. It wasn't going to make me feel more connected to him because the age gap was too significant. He was more than 10 years older than me and that was an age difference that I didn't think I could ever overlook.

"Well, it was nice finding that out about you. You are a cool guy," he said, standing up as he grabbed my hand with his other hand, cupping it with both of them. Roderick was giving me all the support I needed. "And don't you ever bring yourself down because of the people that live in this town. You're going to be fine. I'm sure that you'll eventually find your partner when the moment is right."

"Thanks, but I don't think that it will ever happen, not while I'm still paraplegic."

He retreated both of his hands and then waved his right one.

"Don't worry about that. I'm sure there's someone who likes you for the person you are and that he wants you, too."

CHAPTER 8

Roderick

I was still in his bedroom, feeling like tears were about to come out and that there was nothing I could do about that. I didn't think I was going to find out that he was gay, just like me. He had been hiding that from everyone, including me, this whole time, and the fact that he came out to me meant a lot. Douglas needed all the support that he could get and I was going to give it to him.

After another moment of silence, he pursed his lips before saying, "There is something that I want you to do for me right now, and I hope that you don't think that it's too weird. It means a lot to me."

I perked up my right eyebrow. The way he said that, I could tell that it meant a lot to him, and regardless of what it was, I wanted to fulfill his wish.

"Tell me what it is and I'll do it."

"Thanks. Do you remember the diapers that are in my closet?"

I nodded and then he added, "Could you get one and then put it on me?"

His eyes were holding mine, which was something that he didn't do often anymore. I figured that I was going to find out something even deeper about him, that he was going to reveal a side of his life that was cryptic and curious at the same time, but I didn't think that he was going to ask me to diaper him.

What the hell was going on here?

He must have perceived the confusion on my face because he then said, "I know it's weird, but what's weirder is that you have to take me to the bathroom and then put me on the toilet whenever I have…" He said, his cheeks going beet red. Whenever he had to go to the bathroom and use the toilet, he always felt uncomfortable, mostly because he knew that he was an adult and that his current condition was humiliating. "I just don't want to let that happen. I want to wear diapers so that you don't have to take me to the bathroom every time that I need to shit."

I put both of my hands on my waist, studying Douglas' face.

"I know how it makes you feel, but it doesn't really bother me. I know that it's necessary and, if you are lucky and disciplined, I know that you will get control over your body again."

"Thanks, but in the meantime, I just want to be diapered so that I don't have to worry about that. Not to mention that then it will be a lot easier for you. You won't have to worry about taking me to the bathroom every time that I need to pee or take a shit. I just think that it's more practical."

I took a long breath, taking my hands off my waist. "Sure, whatever you need, but I'm still curious why you have diapers in your closet. You aren't a father, never was one, and your family doesn't come here often."

His cheeks grew redder all of a sudden and I knew that I hit a spot where he was uncomfortable. Nevertheless, this just might be the moment to press on.

"One of my friends was pregnant last year and I was going to give her baby everything that you see in my house, but then we had a fallout and she didn't want me anymore as her friend. I didn't want to give her the items that I bought, and since I couldn't get rid of them, I decided to keep them with me."

"And spread them all over the house? You couldn't keep them stowed in just one place?"

As if to show me that I was wrong about this, his cheeks grew even redder than before. Douglas was almost like a burning furnace and, noticing that, I was almost feeling bad about the questions that I was making. Nevertheless, the moment that we were having was almost like a snowball rolling down a hill. It just couldn't be stopped.

"You've been living with me long enough to know that I'm not a very tidy person. I don't like keeping my house neat and clean. All those things are spread out everywhere because I couldn't be bothered to keep them in the same place."

I blinked twice, not really believing if what he just said made sense. And yet, there was no point in continuing that particular thread of our conversation.

I turned around, made a beeline to the closet, pushed the door to the side, and then grabbed one of the diapers. One of the things that first caught my attention, the first day that I was here, was how big they looked, even for babies born bigger than normal. That was one of the primary reasons why I thought that Douglas was full of shit when he said that these items were gifts for his friend's newborn.

Since he was living in such a terrible condition, I couldn't even bring that up and I couldn't confront him about it. Douglas needed all of my support, I reaffirmed.

I tore open the package wrapped around the diaper, taking it out of it. Tossing the plastic inside the trash can inside his room for recyclable materials, I then spread the diaper on his bed, noticing how cute it looked. It really was big – the size looked big enough even for an adult like him, I registered. He was smaller than most men his age, but still… it was kind of odd that all of his diapers were the right size for him.

Doodles of Mickey covered the exterior of the diaper and the fragrance that came from it was pretty good. I couldn't quite put my finger on what smell it resembled, but I thought that it felt like the smell of chocolate mixed with strawberry and a couple of other things.

"You're going to be smelling pretty nice when I put this on you," I said and he cracked open a smile.

"Thanks, but I hope that doesn't mean you think that I smell bad most of the time."

"Quite the contrary. It's almost like you are the opposite of a magnet for bad smells. You always smell pretty nice, and I make sure of that every day," I joked, brushing my hands over the diaper and then turning it around a couple of times.

"Could you… also grab another one?" Douglas asked.

"Why another one?" I perked up both of my eyebrows. It was already a little curious that he wanted to be diapered as an adult, and now he just added a couple of piles of curiosity on top of that.

"It feels better."

After a second without either of us saying anything, I asked, "Have you done this before?"

Douglas' cheeks went beet-red again.

"I might have," he replied, turning his eyes to the side and then doing everything in his power not to tell me the rest of the truth.

"You might have? Tell me the whole truth this time," I demanded, my tone showing that I wasn't threatening or forcing him to do something that he didn't want to.

Still looking the other way, he responded, "When I realized that they could fit me too, I tried one of them."

"It looks like you might've liked it a bit too much."

"More than once, to be more precise," and then we both started laughing uncontrollably.

When we weren't laughing anymore and were back to being our normal selves, I said, "Well, I have to say that you have good taste for diapers. I can feel how soft it is, and it also looks pretty good. But where did you buy diapers so big?"

"My friends' son was born bigger than most babies, and I think I might have overestimated his size a little. I bought it online. I don't even remember the name of the shop…" Douglas said, his voice lowering a little, though I couldn't put my finger on the why.

Did he just lie to me? I hoped that he didn't, but there was no denying that this whole diaper thing was bringing out a side of him that he didn't want to be talking about right now.

It meant that I was going to see him naked, just like so many times before now, but also that, this time, it was going to be different. Now that I knew he was gay, there was a slight chance that we could become more than what we were right now, even though I didn't think that it was going to happen. Just the possibility that it might was good enough for me.

CHAPTER 9

Douglas

When he said that he was going to diaper me, it was almost like I was dreaming. I couldn't contain my excitement. I didn't goad him into doing this with me, but it was almost like that was what was happening. Roderick just grabbed the other diaper from the closet, tore it open with his fingers, and then tossed the plastic into the trash bin.

He spread it out on the bed as well, his fingers moving from left to right over it, smoothing out the wrinkles.

"He really was a big baby…" I said as if to reaffirm what I stated before.

"He really must've been," Roderick also said, but it was almost like he was mostly murmuring to himself.

"I suppose we should do this now, then."

When he turned around and appeared that he was going to come to me, probably to take my clothes off, I said, "Have you ever done this before?"

He put both of his hands on his waist, letting out a cloud of breath. "No, I never did. This is my first time."

"How do you feel about it?"

"Curious and excited."

I perked up my right eyebrow, my heart speeding up all of a sudden. I thought that he was going to say he felt weirded out, but not that he was curious and excited. Those were the last things, actually, that I thought were going to come out of his mouth.

"Curious and excited?" I asked.

"It's the first time I'm doing it, so of course I'm excited and also curious. I just want to make sure that I'm going to do it right, and so I need to follow whatever tips you might have for me."

"I'm afraid I don't know much about this as well."

"Well, let's watch a video before, then."

I pulled up one side of my lips, finding it amusing what he just said.

"Are there even tutorials on how to do it?"

His hand went into the pocket of his pants and he fished out of it his phone. As he held it in front of him, he said, "It's the Internet. Everything that you need is on it."

"Good point," I said and then he sat down by the side of where I was lying on the bed. I felt the bed sagging and the warmth coming from his body. My eyes went up and down, dissecting the curves of his arms and his bulging biceps. His right arm had a tattoo - the name of someone – and I couldn't help but wonder who that person had been to him.

I wished I could lift my hand and move my fingers around his arm, feeling the firmness of his muscles, but I couldn't even lift my pinky. My body was so traumatizing right now. It made me want to hurt myself, and I only hadn't done that yet because Roderick was with me every time I wanted.

He turned on the screen of his phone and I asked, "Who's Winton?"

He made a noise with his mouth that almost sounded like a complaint, as if he was trying to show me that he didn't want to talk about that, but that now he had. I was curious and if there was something that didn't change about me after the accident, it was my morbid curiosity.

"Someone that I met a long time ago."

"Someone that you met a long time ago? Do you want to talk

about it?”

He lowered his hand that was holding the phone and the screen went black after not being used for a couple of seconds.

“You asked me if I had a partner. I *once* had a partner, someone that I loved, but he hurt me. He hurt me so deeply that I’m still not over it.”

“And yet, you didn’t erase this tattoo.”

“I could get rid of it, but the process is a little too painful and a bit expensive. It isn’t worth it.”

“I know about that, but if you hate Winton that much, then I think it would have been worth it. Keeping the tattoo means having to be reminded of him all the time.”

He turned his head so that he was looking at me confidently. “Maybe I want that. I think I want to be reminded how painful a new relationship can be.”

I cleared my throat, nothing happening in the following seconds. Roderick didn’t say anything and I felt far too uncomfortable to say anything else, even though I wanted to.

What Roderick just said meant that we could probably never become lovers, even though part of me wanted to make that happen. I wanted to give ourselves a chance, to become his boyfriend, especially now that I knew he could become a perfect daddy. He was taking care of me so lovingly that I couldn’t imagine myself spending the next years of my life with someone that wasn’t him.

I didn’t think that Roderick thought the same, but I hoped he did.

“So, that means that you aren’t open to another relationship?” I asked, clearing my throat again. I just had no idea if I was skirting a topic that hurt him so much that he didn’t even want to talk about it, but I was still morbidly curious again. I wanted to go all the way to the bottom of what happened between him and Winton.

“I haven’t thought about that yet.”

“How long has it been since you broke up with him?”

He looked up, thinking, and then lowered his head when he replied, "About five years ago."

"And, during this whole time, you haven't thought about it? You don't even feel anymore that you might want someone else?"

"If I wanted someone else, I would have already known that, don't you think?"

"Good point."

"Why do you want to know so much about that part of my life?"

I swallowed down the lump that was in my throat. I figured that he was going to ask that, but I was still not prepared for it.

"I'm just curious."

"Again? Just like that time when I first met you at that café?"

I nodded once and slowly, showing my uncomfortableness.

"Just like then. I care about you, as much as you care about me. After all, you mean more to me than all of my friends."

He seemed tense before I said that, but now his facial expression softened up.

After he smiled without showing his teeth, he said, "You can be so sweet sometimes. I'm sure you'll find someone that wants to be your boyfriend."

I almost wanted to ask him if that person could be him, but I held that back. I didn't want to make this moment feel more uncomfortable than it already was. And yet, there was one more thing that needed to be cleared up.

"So, do you feel comfortable talking about Winton?"

His eyes studied me for a couple of seconds as he mulled over my question. I had no idea if he was going to talk about that, and answer the questions that I still had for him, but I was hopeful that he was going to be more willing.

"I felt that he was growing more distant over time."

"What do you mean?" I asked, realizing that Roderick was indeed more willing now to talk about the woes of his past and -

what appeared to be - his only relationship.

"He was much younger than me and I thought that we could connect, that we could understand each other, but then he started spending more time with his friends than me, not wanting to watch the same things that I did, or to read the same books that I did, and to complain about my work. He thought that I risked my life unnecessarily."

"Really? You just grew more distant because you couldn't do the same things together anymore?" I asked. I was trying to understand his point of view on his relationship with Winton and I was thinking that I was beginning to get it, even though it was still fuzzy to me.

"Spending time with my loved one is important to me."

"I've always thought that it doesn't really matter, as long as you love him."

He cocked his head before he asked, "What do you mean?"

"Love is what it is. If you love someone, then you love him regardless of what happens, and that nothing can separate you and that it doesn't matter how much time you spend together."

He put his hand on my leg, gliding it up and down.

"It shows that you lack experience when it comes to relationships. I also thought that way when I first fell in love, but then I realized that being with someone, spending time with him, and being physically present with him was important to me. Too much so, in fact."

And Roderick just might be right about that. I was, indeed, beginning to fall in love with him thanks to the amount of time that we were sharing together.

And I didn't think that was wise.

CHAPTER 10

Roderick

I didn't think that Douglas was going to begin asking those questions to me. I had no idea what his angle was, but I was showing that I was willing to answer all of his questions. I supposed that doing that was something that I should've done a long time ago – I mean, confronting that part of my life. What happened between me and Winton was forever going to be ingrained in my mind and there was nothing that could be done about that, other than letting it all out. And who better to do that with than Douglas? He was my best friend now, even though I wanted to make it so he was much more than that, too.

It was just so hard for me, thanks to the age gap. I was pretty sure that his interests were much different from mine, that he liked other things, and that he also preferred spending more time with his friends than with me. Right now, he was doing the opposite because he didn't have another choice, but when he was better, I was pretty sure that it was going to change, and that was something I didn't even want to think about.

It wasn't that he was going to stop being my friend, but that he was going to grow more distant and that I would eventually confront him about that, destroying what we had between us right now.

"Maybe you're right about that."

I didn't say anything and then Douglas added, "If we ever become lovers, I'll make sure that something like that doesn't happen between us."

I bulged my eyes out. I didn't think that that was going to be brought up all of a sudden.

And seeing my reaction, he chuckled before saying, "And don't worry about it. I don't think that we could ever become lovers, even though…"

He trailed off and the seconds passed and he didn't say anything else. His cheeks were beet-red again, showing how uncomfortable he was. I was also feeling extremely awkward right now. I didn't think that our conversation was going to veer in this direction.

"But what if it happened?" I asked, feeling sweat drops coming out of the pores of my skin.

"What do you mean?" Douglas stammered and I had no idea what this meant. I was supposed to diaper him, to put two diapers on him, but things just took an entirely different direction and I could just barely remember the diapers that I left on the other side of the bed.

"We becoming boyfriends…?" Douglas asked again, making me wish that doing that was possible, that I could find a way to love in his heart, but knowing that I couldn't. I was unable to make amends and compromises with Winton when it happened, after all.

I just didn't want to go through the same painful process where I learned that the differences between us were too great to be managed.

"I wouldn't be opposed to that idea," I still said, my voice lower all of a sudden.

He didn't know what to say, clearing up his throat. Everything around us was quiet and I'd be able to hear a pin dropping on the floor if it happened.

"But you just said that it still hurts you too much, what happened between you and Winton."

"It still does, but…" I chuckled, standing up and going to the other side of the bed. "I know that it won't happen. You need to live your own life, recover, and spend time with your friends. You won't need me when you are better."

"That's not true. Even if and when I'm walking again, I'll still want to be with you. Even if you move away, I'll always remember you."

His words warmed up my heart, making me imagine what my life would be like if I was his boyfriend, always loving him, always doing everything to make him feel better, and buying everything he wanted. He had some odd habits, like the things with the diapers and wearing a bib when eating, but that was what made him different.

"I know…" I said, pulling the comforter off him and then pulling down his pants and underwear. It wasn't the first time that I saw his cock and scrotum but, this time, it was different. His cock was slightly bigger than normal, which meant that he was feeling turned on. I didn't know if that meant he thought that I was his type, but I was still a little surprised and disconcerted. I didn't think that it was going to happen. During all the times when I bathed him or just took off his clothes for another purpose, he never had an erection.

"I'm sorry. I didn't mean for this to happen," he said, referencing his erection.

"No, it's okay. You can't really control it, though I feel flattered that you think I'm hot."

He cleared his throat, saying, "Well, you are."

For a moment, I didn't know what to say. Douglas just confirmed that he had a crush on me, and that was good news and bad news at the same time. Him having a crush on me opened so many doors, but I was also afraid of stepping through them.

I eventually chuckled, saying, "I've always thought the same. Since that first time we met, I've been thinking about you, always remembering your face, your mannerisms, the things that you do only the way you can, the tone of your voice, and pretty much everything else about you."

"You're almost making me think that we could really become more than what we are."

I didn't say anything, pushing back the tears that wanted to come out. I wasn't going to cry and especially not in front of the only person that needed to see that I was strong.

Changing the subject, I said, "Well, it's time to diaper you, don't you think?"

His eyes lit up when he heard that. "Yes, that would be nice, but aren't you going to watch a YouTube tutorial first?"

I thought about it for a second before responding, "No, I don't think that's going to be necessary. Putting a diaper on you shouldn't be that hard, right?"

After a moment, I said, "And I guess that first I should take you off the bed."

I looped my arms around him, pulling him up and then putting him in his wheelchair. It was something that soon he wasn't going to need. I figured that he felt quite uncomfortable naked and in the wheelchair, but I was going to fix that in a bit.

I cleared his bed, spread the first diaper on it, and then picked him up in my arms. He was light, but not too much. I still had to exert some effort when hoisting him and I had to do that gently so that there was no chance he could get hurt.

"I'm so excited. This is the first time that I'm getting diapered."

"It's just a temporary solution, though. When you are back to being your normal self again, you won't need it."

Douglas was almost showing that he wanted to say something, but whatever it was, he kept it hidden from me.

I settled him on the diaper and then brought cream for his skin and a little bit of talcum, which was also in a bottle. I spread the cream on my hands and then on his sensitive parts, making sure that I wasn't turning him on much more than he was. I didn't want to give him the wrong impression regarding my intentions.

I mean, Douglas was still my crush, but I wasn't going to do anything sexual with him unless he wanted to.

After that, I wiped my hands clean and then grabbed the bottle of talcum. I tossed some of it over his lower parts, making sure that it was spread over everything.

Following that, I pulled the sides of the diaper and then snapped them together, making sure that they were well-connected. Then, I slid the second diaper underneath him and secured it around him as well.

After that was done, he was diapered – twice.

"So, what do you think of it?" I asked, putting both of my hands on my waist as I admired my work. Douglas looked just like a true baby boy, which was… endearing and sweet.

"It's incredible. I feel so safe right now. You did an amazing job, especially for someone that didn't have much experience with this."

"Well, I'm happy with that, then."

CHAPTER 11

After Roderick diapered me for the first time, it became a common occurrence between us. He diapered me every day from now on. It was just that much more convenient and faster for him when he needed to clean me. Not to mention that he actually enjoyed the whole process that came with him diapering me.

As a little, I was loving this turn in our lives. I wanted to make it permanent, even after I was back to being my normal self. The therapies were working and I was beginning to regain the movement of my legs and arms. And yet, it was going to take time until I was back at a hundred percent.

I had a pacifier in my mouth this time. When I asked Roderick to put it in my mouth, I knew he was going to find it weird and that he was going to have several questions for me, but he still did it without making a big fuss about it.

I suckled on the pacifier greedily, not wanting to take it out of my mouth for anything.

We were in my bedroom. We didn't sleep in the same bedroom, even though I wanted to make it so we did. I knew it was never going to happen, so I wasn't pumping my hopes up that it would.

We were more intimate now, but I was still just his friend and I had no idea if that was ever going to change.

Roderick had his arm draped over my shoulder, and the warmth of his body was around me, pulsing against me. It was dark outside and a light rain painted the trees and the lawn, making a gentle and constant noise too, but it was almost unnoticeable. It added to the atmosphere around us. It was also getting a little cold now that the seasons were shifting. We were entering the Fall season, so temperatures were going to keep dropping.

Roderick had nothing more than his trousers and a shirt on. The shirt was white and the right size for his body. It delineated his muscles and how rippling they were. Being paraplegic didn't mean that I couldn't get hard, I remembered. I could still get hard – I just couldn't do anything about it. All these months and I hadn't even masturbated again yet, and I didn't think that I would anytime soon.

I also had little on in terms of clothes, wearing nothing more than a shirt and my diaper. Roderick diapered me again tonight and I felt ready to sleep, especially because the movie that we were watching, which was Cinderella, wasn't attention-grabbing.

Roderick lifted his arm and checked the watch on his wrist.

"It's almost 11. Don't you think that you should go to sleep?"

It was the first time that he brought up something like that. The more time that I lived with Roderick, the more I started to think that he was a Daddy. I was almost mustering up enough courage to ask him about that, but I didn't know if I could take that risk. What if he got so angry at me that he decided to leave me? I didn't know if that was the most likely outcome, but I was, again, morbidly curious.

I still couldn't move my hands freely like before, so when I tried and he realized that I wanted to take out of my mouth the pacifier that was in it, he did that for me.

And when I could speak, I wetted my throat and said, "Really? This is a first between us."

"Your classes are online now, but you still need to study and be diligent about it. Otherwise, you won't graduate."

I narrowed my eyes slightly, giving him a judging look. We both then started laughing uncontrollably, the room suddenly feeling a lot busier. Moments later, when we both stopped laughing, I said, "How about giving me one more hour? Until the movie ends."

"Do you think you deserve the extra hour? Do you think that you've been good recently?"

I nodded once and frantically, giving him a big and bright smile.

After that laugh and our initial and bright conversation, I made a decision. I was ready to tackle that challenge and I didn't think that the consequences were going to be negative. I knew that Roderick was a man with an open mind. I knew that so much that it was no surprise that he had been doing all the little/Big things with me without making a big fuss about it.

After a moment of silence, when all I could hear was the rain falling outside and the sounds coming from the TV, I asked, "Roderick… Are you a Daddy?"

He turned his head to me slowly, scrunching up his eyebrows.

"A Daddy? What do you mean about that? I already told you that I'm gay and that I had only one boyfriend. I'm pretty sure that he isn't pregnant with my baby, if that's what you are inferring. A man can't get pregnant, last time I checked."

I shook my head and curled up the right side of my lips.

"That's not what I mean."

He intensified the scrunching up of his eyebrows.

"And what is it that you mean? I'm honestly confused."

"Pause the movie."

And after I said that, he picked up the remote and pressed the red button, the screen freezing. If everything around us was quiet before, now it was even more so.

"And get your phone. There's something that I need to show you."

To say that I was nervous about this was a huge understatement. I was terrified about telling Roderick the truth about me, what finally tied everything together. He was finally going to find out that I was a little. It was disappointing that he wasn't a Daddy, but that was okay.

He grabbed his phone and turned it on.

As he waited for my next command, I said, "Look up 'ABDL.'"

I thought he was going to, but then he turned off the screen of the phone, putting it back on his lap. I could feel his body touching against mine, which was such a huge turn-on that I was glad that the comforter hid my erection from his curious eyes.

"I don't think I need to do that. I want you to tell me what's going on."

I blinked twice, not understanding what he meant by that. Was Roderick figuring everything out by himself?

"Why?"

"I think it's better that you tell me straight out of your mouth."

I cleared my throat, my heart thundering in my chest.

"Please tell me that you aren't going to get angry at me. I wouldn't be able to live with myself if you did."

He grabbed my hand, brushing his thumb over it.

"I would never do that. Even after Wilton broke up with me, I never hated him. It won't be different with you."

I let out a deep sigh, saying, "Alright. I'm going to explain everything to you, and I hope that you do good on your word."

Moments later, I was still in the same bedroom, with the same guy, in the same bed, and with his arm still around my shoulders. I looked up, finding his eyes and noticing how watery they were. It wasn't that he was crying, but that he was now feeling a little sensitive after the bomb of truths that I just dropped.

"I did some research before you told me about that. I started to look up some things about age play, but I didn't think that it was what was going on between us."

I perked up, noticing that I could finally move my body a little, but not sufficiently. It was still a far cry from who I was before the accident.

"So, you kind of knew about it all along."

"Something like that, though I still thought that I was just hallucinating it."

"And? What are we going to do now?"

"You tell me. I'm here to do everything you want and to make sure that you're happy. It's not going to change anything on my end. As far as I know, I'm still going to be diapering you every morning and night, feeding you, putting a bib on your neck, and everything else. It matters that you are a little, but our dynamics won't change."

What he just said relieved me, but it was still not enough. And yet, that meant that another door opened between us and I wanted to take advantage of it. I wanted to step through it and find out what it had, what it hid from me.

"Does that mean that you aren't against us taking things a level higher?"

He shook his head and said, "I'm not, but you will essentially have to walk me through it."

I smiled, nodding. "I'm okay with that."

I heard the tree's branch scraping against the window, reminding me that time didn't stop and that I was still here.

"So, what do you want to do?"

"I want to become your little and you to become my Daddy. I want to pretend that I'm a baby again, that I don't even need to talk, and that you control every aspect of my life. I want to give myself entirely to you."

His eyes were holding my gaze, looking deeply through it. I noticed his head dipping and then our lips connected, and I finally kissed for the first time. My dick was hard and raging under my trousers, poking against the comforter, and it was perfect. It just felt fitting. It was a passionate kiss, but also dangerously slow.

Then, Roderick pulled his head back, asking, "How was that for a first kiss?"

CHAPTER 12

Roderick

It was amazing. That's what Douglas told me and I believed him. Everything was developing perfectly between us and that old wound that I thought couldn't be healed now was. I could imagine myself having another relationship and I knew that we were making it official. I was his Daddy and he was my little.

We were just walking out of the hospital and Douglas looked jubilant, almost swinging his arms and legs, moving them as fast as he could, and walking with me quite amusingly. He could almost hop around me, his hand holding mine for a few moments until he remembered that we were still in Hope River, where almost everyone was conservative and they would scrunch their noses up if they found two men being intimate with each other.

"Ooopsie, shouldn't have done that," Douglas joked, shooting his hand to his mouth and covering it. He giggled but he stifled it. When he lowered his head and we were by the side of my car, he added, "I promise I won't do that again."

We were still in the fall season, the trees' leaves falling to the ground and the trees themselves changing drastically. They lost most of their leaves, and the atmosphere of the city lost a little bit of its charm.

And yet, the only thing that mattered to me right now was the fact that my little - I was still getting used to thinking of him that way – was happy and almost like his old self again.

"I'm getting so much better. I can almost walk and do everything I used to."

I opened the door for him and he sat down in the seat, putting on his seatbelt.

I sat in my seat behind the steering wheel, turning on the car seconds later. I drove him home and then opened the door for him. He stepped out of the vehicle, hurried over to the porch of his house, and opened the door. Douglas didn't need his wheelchair anymore, which was excellent. And yet, I couldn't help but feel a hint of sadness in my heart. It was almost like I could see that everything around us was changing.

And then, suddenly, he dashed up the stairs, going to his bedroom. I was just stepping inside the house after closing the car's door when I noticed him doing that.

I had no idea what was going on in his mind, but it was certainly something that I didn't expect from him. We had our own rules and punishments that needed to be delivered when he was being naughty. They were written on a blackboard that hung from a wall in the living room, where he could always check it in case he forgot something important.

Douglas came thundering down the stairs, holding a paint bucket in his left hand and a paintbrush in his right one. He opened a big, brief smile on his face, giggling as he dashed over to the other side of the living room, where he started to paint one of the walls.

My hands went to my head, running over to him at that same moment. I knew that Douglas was naughty, that he could do things that didn't make sense and that he liked breaking the rules sometimes, but I didn't think that he was going to pull something like that on me, especially after today when he made such huge progress on regaining the movement of his arms and legs.

It wasn't that I was pissed he was painting the wall of the living room without my permission, ruining the original paint, but that he was doing something that the doctor advised him not to do – and that was running around and moving carelessly. That was dangerous and could lead to him regressing when it came to his progress.

I pulled him by the collar of his shirt and he fell on his ass on the floor, the bucket tumbling over and spreading the paint all over, making me widen my eyes. I was now even more irritated than before. It was going to take me forever until I cleaned the floor.

He dropped the paintbrush that was in his hand, adding to the mess that he was making.

"What the hell do you think you're doing, little Doug?" I hissed, letting my tone of voice transmit my anger.

His happy smile faded and he lost his initial energy, saying, "goo-goo, dah dah?" Which was just like him, especially when he was being little and also when he was naughty.

When he was little, he was like a baby and pretended that he couldn't speak, which was perfect for someone that was in trouble right now. He made a huge mess in the living room, paint was all over the floor, and it was going to be a mess until I finished cleaning it.

I waggled my finger in front of me, determining that whatever he was thinking he was doing right now wasn't going to work on me.

His face assumed a disappointed tone, which I expected from him.

I put my hands under his armpits and hoisted him up until he was back on his feet, but then a moment later he fell back to his knees, crawling around me as he kept on saying, "goo-goo, dah dah" and making other silly baby noises.

I picked him up and he threw his arms and legs around me, looking at me with amusing eyes. I narrowed my eyes slightly, patting his back.

"I'm not going to change my mind about this. You know what

the rules say and what your punishment should be."

Little Doug said 'goo-goo, dah dah" again, but he truly wasn't going to fool me. I went to the couch while he was still glued to me and I sat down on it. I spread him over my lap and then lowered his diaper, exposing his butt.

Now that he was better, he could feel again everything that happened to his body. My hand roamed over his butt, feeling it. He could feel that too and the hint of pleasure that his eyes showed couldn't be hidden. If anything, it was seeping out.

He moaned softly when I lifted my hand, almost sounding like he was complaining about what I was going to do. We had our safeword and he could stop this anytime he wanted, though I was pretty sure that he wasn't going to. When it came to role-playing, he was always adamant about going through with it until the end. I guess it was something that was just part of him.

"I know this is going to hurt, but I know you love it as well," and just as I finished saying that, I dropped my hand on his butt, slapping it. He winced and tears formed at the corners of his eyes, but the smile that crept up on his face was telling.

Little Doug was asking for more and I was more than willing to give him what he wanted.

I slapped his ass several times in a row, making sure that the message was delivered, but that the punishment served a deeper purpose, too. I just wanted to teach him that naughty things were always going to be punished, regardless of how cute he looked.

Moments later, when the punishment was finally over, he slid off my lap and hugged my legs, burying his head in them. He was crying gently, but he wasn't sobbing or doing anything else that might indicate that he wasn't comfortable with what just happened.

I picked him up gently and nestled him on my lap again, letting his arms go around me and hug me. After some minutes, he stopped crying and I pulled his head back so that I could look at his face. Brushing my fingers over his cheeks, I cleared away his tears and he cooed against my chest, and I let him do it without doing anything else.

Everything was better than it was before and it was calm and peaceful around me.

Could things get any better than they were? I didn't know, but I was curious to see what the future held in store for me and also for my little Doug.

CHAPTER 13

Douglas

Now that I could finally walk, kick, swing my arms around, and live joyfully like before, everything was so much better that I just couldn't stop grinning. I was always with a big, bright smile on my face that went from my right ear to my left ear, showing just how exuberant I was.

As usual, I was with a diaper on, a pacifier in my mouth, and wore nothing else. I was watching Dragon Ball Z on TV and Goku was already giving his all against Vegeta. If there was a cartoon – that was actually an anime – that wasn't from Disney and that I loved, it was Dragon Ball Z. It always reminded me of my childhood years, when I could sit in front of a TV and do nothing, just binge-watching one episode after the other, thinking about nothing. The only thing that would then be in my mind was what I would watch afterward.

I was so tense right now because it appeared that Vegeta was winning and Goku was losing. Like, I didn't know what was happening, but Goku already fired up his Kaioken times three and was truly giving his all, his clothes ripped and torn, but he was still not making much progress in terms of winning the battle.

As a huge Goku fan, I couldn't help but feel so tense that I was clutching my little stuffie tightly in my hand, digging my fingers into it. I knew that I was hurting him, but I also wasn't thinking straight right now. The little stuffie was pressed up against my chest, buried in it.

My Daddy was on the couch, his hand flipping the page of a newspaper. He was old school like that, preferring paper newspapers over the digital version. When he wasn't working, he was always checking out the local news, like he was doing now. Everything around us was quiet, other than the noise that the coffee machine was making as it prepared his coffee.

The coloring book was on the floor and in front of me, and the sketch was half-colored. I was still working on it and should be finished with it soon. In the meantime, I was focused on the battle between Goku and Vegeta. I knew who was going to win in the end, but that wasn't the point.

Seeing Vegeta slamming Goku against the ground, my frustration rose up in me, making me pluck out of my mouth my pacifier and hurl it against the wall opposite to me, from where it then fell to the floor.

Nothing happened in the following seconds, but I was pretty sure that Big Roderick noticed that. So much so that I then heard him grumbling something, as if he was considering punishing me right now.

I didn't say anything as I crawled over to the pacifier, picked it up, and turned it around in my hand. It was a beautiful pacifier featuring Piccolo from Dragon Ball Z on the front side, right behind the teat.

I put it in my mouth again, but then when I felt the rashness and the dustiness of the dirt and whatever else was on it, I plucked it out of my mouth and dropped it on the floor.

Big Roderick grumbled something under his breath again, and I knew that what I just did was another infraction. The only problem was that I had no idea if he was willing to go through with the punishment that he was already considering.

I knew that my punishments were also based on how many infractions I committed, after all.

But since the pacifier was dirty and cleaning it right now

wasn't an option, I decided to return to my original position behind the coloring book. I grabbed another crayon and started to rub the tip of it on the paper over and over, painting between the lines and making little progress.

I knew that I had Daddy's attention on me and that he was watching me closely. He was watching me closer than before, pondering if he should punish me right now. I could look at the blackboard above the TV and see what the punishment was for different infractions in a row, but I didn't want to do that. It would only make me feel more anxious.

Seconds later, Big Roderick said, "Shouldn't you be with your pacifier in your mouth?"

I turned my head toward him and even though I missed my pacifier, I wasn't going to put it in my mouth unless it was clean. I said 'goo-goo, dah dah' and made other funny baby noises to highlight that I was still in my little headspace and that, no matter what happened now, nothing was going to take me out of it.

Big Roderick shuffled over to the pacifier on the floor, picked it up, and checked it out with his eyes. "Ohhh, look at this. It's so dirty."

When he turned his eyes back to me, I smiled from ear to ear. I was hoping that my happy face was going to deter him from choosing a punishment for me. Sometimes, it wasn't spanking, but other times when I said something that he didn't like and was an insult or just a bad word that I used, he rubbed bath soap on my tongue, which was always nasty.

"Do you think that I'm going to overlook that?" He asked, walking toward me and then crouching, holding the pacifier between me and him.

I just shook my head and continued rubbing the crayon on the page, hoping that it was painting between the lines. My eyes weren't looking down at it, so I had no idea if I was coloring it right or not.

"Goo-goo, dah dah," I said again, my voice impish and a little high-pitched, but only because I truly was in my little headspace and it was where I felt most comfortable.

"I don't like it when you are so rebellious," Daddy said, lifting his right hand and pointing with his finger toward the corner by my side. My body froze up. I knew what that meant and I wasn't ready for it.

"Goo-goo, dah dah?" I said again, but he just shook his head once and I knew that that was the end of it. When Big Roderick had his mind set on something, he never changed it.

My smile faded before I pouted, trying to look sad and bring out the good side of him, his forgiving side, which I knew was there, but he then shook his head again once and determinedly, and I knew I had no choice.

Without a second thought, I crawled over to the corner of the room and sat on the floor with my legs crossed under me.

"You know the rules. When you commit several infractions in a row and pretend that you didn't, you get a timeout. This time, you'll be in this corner for thirty minutes. Only then will you be able to go back to your coloring book."

I widened my eyes for a fraction of a moment, but then they returned to normal when I realized that it was better to go on with the punishment that he was choosing for me. It was better to do that because he had full control over me and I respected him a lot.

Roderick walked away from me after lowering his hand, going back to sitting on the couch before he picked up his newspaper. He flipped another page and continued to read whatever he thought was so important and attention-catching. I didn't know what it was that he found so interesting in reading newspapers, but it wasn't like I could truly understand it anyway.

I was so bored and it hadn't even been five minutes since the timeout started. I was still at the same place, doing nothing, just looking at the corner and trying not to fidget much. I was usually hyperactive and impatient, especially because I just regained full control over my body and could do anything, including running around unhinged.

Minutes later, I couldn't help but peek over my shoulder to see what was happening, to see if Daddy was still reading his newspaper, but then I noticed that he just turned his eyes to me and caught me doing that. I was a little shocked, so much so that I quickly snapped my head back in the other direction so that I was staring straight into the corner of the room.

My blood froze up. I never thought that Big Roderick was always so attentive to the things surrounding him that he knew when I wasn't looking in the direction that he directed me to.

This wasn't going to be easy for me, I thought.

And yet, more minutes passed and when I was already growing frustrated, a hand settled on my shoulder and I snapped my head up. I quickly found out that it was Daddy that was behind me, and could it have been anyone else? Of course not, I thought.

"Your timeout is over and you can now go back to your coloring book. I permit it."

Phew. That was relieving, but that timeout would forever remain in my mind, I was sure of it.

CHAPTER 14

Roleplaying with my little - something that I was still getting used to - was great. It fitted me. I thought that it was going to be strange in the beginning, but then it quickly grew on me and I soon found myself discovering several new things regarding the kink and other aspects behind it. It was endearing, pretty cute, and always extremely rewarding. So much so that I couldn't imagine myself with someone else, doing anything that wasn't protecting little Doug and spanking and inflicting other punishments on him when needed. I was trying to be a firm, determined, and caring Daddy for him, and so that was imperative.

That same day when he was put in a timeout, he came to me without having to ask me if he should do that or not. He had crawled over to me and then, with his lips still pouting slightly, he told me that he regretted everything that he did wrong without using words. It was a little strange at first, but then I soon picked up exactly what was going on.

I just patted him on the head and then on his shoulder, telling him that he could go back to doing his things. He did that with a smile on his face, which warmed me. It was always so excitedly good to see him happy.

But tonight was different. He was on my lap, with his diaper on and a pacifier in his mouth. We were watching a different cartoon this time on the TV in his bedroom – Ben 10. It was still just his bedroom and not a nursery, I thought, feeling somewhat unhappy. I wanted to turn it into one, but I hadn't yet found someone capable enough to build a crib for him. I was pretty sure that I was going to find someone that was a perfectionist when it came to building things with wood and with a couple of other things, but for now, I was still clueless.

Doug was double-diapered, just like the first time I diapered him, which was excellent at making me remember all the good things that happened during that day. It was the prelude to when he told me the truth about him and I was always going to remember that.

The TV's audio was set to low, so much so that I could hear the suckling sounds of the pacifier in his mouth. Little Doug had his head resting on my shoulder and the fact that his body barely moved told me that he was so comfortable that he couldn't imagine himself doing anything else right now. And despite all the differences between us, Doug also couldn't imagine his life without me, which was certainly something that I held dear in my heart.

I brushed my hand over his forehead, then threaded my fingers in his hair.

"Don't you want to sleep already?" I asked, knowing that he wasn't going to respond. Not by using words, anyway.

Little Doug shook his head, continuing to watch Ben 10 on the TV. He liked that cartoon so much that he made me buy several shirts for him featuring its main protagonist. They weren't expensive, but even if they were, it would have been worth it.

His ass, pressed down on my crotch, meant that it was difficult for me not to have an erection right now. In fact, I could already feel the beginnings of it. This whole time, we hadn't done anything sexual yet, which was a pity. I thought about doing that before, but I had no idea if Little Doug was okay with it.

Did he want to lose his virginity? I was clueless about that, but I was pretty sure that soon I was going to find out the truth.

I checked my wristwatch when my eyes widened, noticing that it was already midnight. My little one was supposed to go to sleep at about 10. If he didn't go to sleep at the right time, he always woke up the next morning feeling groggy and was never his usual self. The reason for that was that his biological clock was different from mine and he always woke up thanks to any different noise that his ears heard.

"I think it's about time you went to sleep, don't you think?" I insisted, brushing my hand over his chin, feeling how soft and smooth his skin was.

He didn't shake just his head this time, but also his entire body. It was like it was the beginning of a tantrum, and I sure as hell hoped that wasn't the case. If he threw a tantrum right now, I knew that the punishment would be severe. So much so that it could turn into something sexual.

"Don't throw a tantrum right now. I won't forgive you if you do that."

But then he just shook his body against my arms again, looking and sounding more rebellious, especially thanks to the noises and the sounds coming out of his mouth. It was like he really was trying to piss me off.

"Do you want to be punished? Because this is how you get punished," I warned, hoping that it was going to be enough to set him straight, but I had no idea if he was going to be more willing to listen this time. Especially after regaining full control over his body, being able to move his legs and arms around freely, he was always more rebellious than when he was paraplegic.

And then, suddenly, he lurched away from me, scooting over the bed and crawling away from me as fast as he could. My eyes bulged out and I didn't even know what was happening. All I knew was that he was giggling and had a huge smile on his face. He was happy with what he was doing, but I was worried. I felt like he was losing his respect for me.

I grabbed him by his shoulder, pulled him back until he was sitting on my crotch again, his diaper pressing against my cock and balls. It wasn't that I was planning on making this sexual, but that it was happening naturally. I was hard. I couldn't hide my excitement and erection and I was pretty sure that my shaft was hard enough for him to feel it through the diaper. So much so that Little Doug even peeked over his shoulder, widening his smile.

I moved my hands around his shoulder, making sure that I was signaling that he was under my full control and that he could do nothing about that. If he tried dashing away from me like he just did, then we were going to have more problems than we already had.

I lowered my hand, sneaking it under his diaper. I grabbed his cock as I noticed that he was also already hard. It was a little surprising at first, but I soon brushed that thought away. Now that we were boyfriends, he didn't have to hide anything from me. I was pretty sure that he was also thinking it was about time he lost his virginity to me, even though I was pretty sure that it wasn't going to happen now.

I started to stroke his shaft slowly, moving my hand up and down along its length. He was a little bigger than I thought, but nowhere as big as I was. I was massive, though I didn't like to boast about it. Little Doug caught a sneak peek of my dick one time when I came out of the bathroom and then he told me that I was the biggest guy that he'd seen, porn movies included. He'd also had sneak peeks of some of his friends, I remembered.

I took the pacifier out of his mouth and said, "You can say whatever you want right now. You don't need to be in your little headspace while we are doing this."

He breathed slowly, still with his head turned toward me. Doug made a little movement with it that suggested that he wanted me to kiss him and me being me, I just had to do that. I touched my lips to his, a jolt of pleasure shooting in my body.

"One more," he pleaded and I just waggled my finger in front of him, showing that I wasn't going to do what he wanted. After all, what was happening here was part of the punishment.

"Then, what are you going to do?" Little Doug asked and I

replied by lowering his diaper, exposing his little pee-pee, and my hand looped around it. He was so hard that the skin was a little reddish, something that I didn't think I was going to see tonight. I thought that tonight was going to be just like all other nights, where he behaved himself.

"Something that's going to surprise you," I said, stroking his shaft more violently, picking up the pace and making him think that he was going to come, that he was going to reach his climax, but then stopping when his breathing quickened and his body was beginning to shake.

When Little Doug noticed what was happening, he looked me in the eye and asked, "Why did you do that? It was horrible. It's making me feel so sad."

He pouted, showing his disappointment. Nevertheless, it wasn't going to work on me.

"It's part of the punishment. You threw a tantrum, which should be punished."

"But the punishment for tantrums is different from orgasm denial," he pointed out and he was right. But there was also something that I wrote in small letters, just under all the rules, which was pretty vital, especially for this moment.

"I know that, but it's also true that I can come up with different punishments for the same naughty things that you do."

"That's not fair," he said and I had to respond to that by stroking his shaft again, making him close his eyes halfway and part his lips.

"Whether it's fair or not, I'm going through with it. I'm not going to finish this until it's over and you learn that you shouldn't throw tantrums."

Still moving my hand over his shaft, fast this time, it took little time until he was almost reaching his orgasm. And I stopped stroking his dick soon after that, making sure that he wasn't quite there.

The disappointment on his face was almost palpable. He

wanted to punish me, to slap my face, but he wasn't even going to try doing any of those things. He pouted again, wishing that I wasn't hell-bent on punishing him right now.

"I hate this so much," he said, moving his arms around me and nesting his head on my shoulder. "And I'm so sorry that I threw a tantrum."

I patted his shoulder, massaging his neck with my hand until he calmed down and was feeling better.

"It's okay. As long as you learn from the punishments and that you shouldn't break the rules as often as you do, everything's going to be fine."

And he knew that. It wasn't that he forgave me for the punishments inflicted on him, but that he was comfortable with everything we did. So much so that he already fell asleep.

I was just so sure that our lives, from now on, were going to be filled with happiness, dreams coming true, and our connection growing stronger. Could it get any better? I didn't know, but I was pretty sure that there was a good chance it might.

CHAPTER 15

Roderick

I pulled over, turning off the engine of the car, and then I opened the door. I stepped outside, looking around and checking out Douglas' house. The light in the living room told me that he was already awake. When I left early for work, he was still sleeping. He was such a sleepyhead and always overslept, especially when he didn't go to sleep before 10 PM.

Those were just some of the things I liked about Doug, so I didn't hold them against him. If anything, they made me feel more connected to him, more willing to spend the rest of my life with him regardless of what happened.

Something that started to happen these last few weeks was concerning me, though. It was the fact that now that he had control over his body and could run around and jump and hop around without his legs failing him, his friends were starting to come over here more frequently. I started to try to like them, to be like them, but it was difficult. The age gap was too significant and we both liked different things. They couldn't mingle with me and I couldn't do the same with them. It was for that reason that whenever they were here, I didn't do much more than saying 'hi' to them before quickly retreating to any spot in the house where I felt more comfortable. I always waited until they were out so that I could do the things that I wanted to do with my little one.

He still hadn't come out to them. They didn't think that it

was weird that I was still spending so much time with him, even though I was a police officer and I worked protecting the town, and that was okay.

I walked over to the porch of the house and opened the door after noticing that his friends' cars were parked in the driveway, a fact that already saddened me. I was going to have to pretend again that I was like them, that I was having fun with them, and that I could be their friend even though I was going to be waiting until they were out, like usual.

I opened the door to the living room and stepped in. Douglas and his friends were seated on the floor, forming a circle. They were playing some kind of game on their phones, snapping selfies and photos, recording videos for TikTok, and doing plenty of other things that I couldn't connect with.

I didn't even like taking photos of myself. That was just the way I was and it was going to remain like that until I was dead, I thought.

It took them a while to notice that I was in the living room, but when they noticed it, they waved their hands over their heads, smiling broadly. I did the same, though it was much more restrained. It was difficult to show any excitement when there wasn't any. I had no idea if they noticed that, but they were soon back to what they were doing, thumbing the screens of their phones, cracking jokes, chatting loudly, and snapping photos of themselves.

I sighed, finding my little one and realizing that he was also having fun with them. He was doing the same things that they were and I could see the same thing that happened between me and Wilton taking place here as well. I hoped that it wasn't the case, but I couldn't be sure. So much so that I pushed that thought out of my mind, going to the kitchen, where I sat on one of the stools.

The day passed and then came the day after that and I found myself in the same situation, noticing that Douglas was spending less time with me. He only needed me when he needed to be diapered and when he wanted to role-play. In all other cases, at other times of the day, he spent more time with his friends and doing other things that I didn't find fun.

I tried to bring that up to him, but I didn't know how he was going to take it. I was just hopeful that he wasn't losing interest in me, that he still loved me, that I was just as important to him as I was when he was paraplegic, but I had no idea if that was the case.

More days passed, even weeks, and nothing changed for the better. If anything, things started to get worse. Douglas started to watch things that I had no interest in, started to go out with his friends, sometimes not even coming back home so that I could tuck him under his comforter. I was beginning to lose interest, too. I stopped hunting for a place that could build a crib for him and was beginning to think that the whole age play thing was nothing more than a fling, something that he could toss away when he didn't need it anymore.

There was even a day when I didn't visit him, thinking that he was going to text me right away, asking hurriedly and confusedly what was going on with me, but it didn't happen. He didn't even send me any texts and, the next day, when I showed up at his house, he made no questions about that. It was like Douglas didn't even notice that we didn't talk for a whole day.

I figured that enough was enough and so, one day, when I finished putting a new diaper on him, which was something that I could still enjoy about our relationship, I decided to confront him.

I sat by his side on the bed while he was still watching TV and thumbing the screen of his phone fervently before asking, "Douglas, do you still love me?"

The next moment, he didn't say anything, still just thumbing the screen of his phone, smiling, and acting like he didn't even hear me, which was disconcerting and heartbreaking.

I nudged his shoulder with my hand until he finally snapped his head to me, showing anger on his face.

"Don't you see that I'm busy?" He hissed and I didn't like the tone that he used. It made me think that he really wasn't in love with me and that my presence here meant nothing to him.

"I'm trying to talk to you. These last few months, you've been different. You've changed and I don't like that."

He cocked up his eyebrow, looking at me confusedly.

"I haven't changed. It's you that can't seem to fit in with my friends."

"I'm the one that can't fit in with your friends?" I asked, standing up and trying not to look too angry. "I'm trying, but I can't. I'm not here for them. I'm here for you and because you are the most important person to me in my life."

"I don't see what's the problem. They come here sometimes, we have fun, and then you look all broody, standing in a corner and not interacting with us. Frankly, I'm getting tired of that."

I shook my head, going to the door and opening it. Douglas wasn't even looking at my face, which was telling. I waited to see if he was going to say anything else and he didn't, which wasn't surprising.

"If you want me to leave, just say so."

Douglas didn't say anything and I turned around, walking to the first floor and then out of the house. I looked behind me as I waited to see if he was going to come jumping out of his house, but nothing happened. I was pretty sure that he was still lying in his bed and texting with his friends.

A tear came out and I brushed it away with the back of my hand. No point in crying right now. I felt this coming a mile away. I knew that it was going to happen. Douglas had a life of his own before I showed up in it and he only needed me for as long as he needed to go through his therapies and make his body better.

Now that he was back to being his old self, he didn't want me to continue being his Daddy.

DOUGLAS' EPILOGUE

I woke up the next morning hoping that I was going to be cradled in his arms, but finding it unsurprising that he wasn't in the bed. The bed was cold and unwelcoming, making me groan. I turned slightly to the side as I noticed that, outside, the sun was hidden behind the clouds. The sky was white and gray, overcast, and it appeared that, soon, snowflakes were going to be falling from it and painting the landscape.

I was supposed to be excited about the change of seasons, but I wasn't. Without my daddy and knowing the things that I did, I felt I was to blame for the way that he just walked out on me without saying anything else.

My phone was on the nightstand and I grabbed it, pulling up the screen where his contact number was. I pondered messaging him, but I thought that that was the wrong thing to do. If all he got from me was a message saying that I was sorry for the way I acted, he would probably feel that I should be blamed even more than he was already doing against me.

I didn't like that at all and so I considered doing the next thing, which was even better than the first one at getting what I wanted. I considered calling him, not knowing if he was going to take that well as well. What if it angered him more than he already was?

I didn't have the answer to that question, and I knew that something – anything – needed to be done as soon as possible.

It was early in the morning and he should be working, though that wasn't an impediment. In Hope River, nothing happened anyway and I was pretty sure that he was just seated in his patrol car, doing nothing. He didn't even need a partner, I remembered. And minutes later, I finally made up my mind.

I pressed the button to call him, hoping that he was going to pick up the call right away, but finding it unsurprising when he didn't. The phone continued the call, trying to make him pick it up, but nothing happened. It was like he was trying to ignore me, which was to be expected. I was the one ignoring him this whole time, which made me feel terrible about myself.

He spent so much time with me, so much effort to make me feel better, and he also paid for all my therapies and everything else needed to heal my body, and then I just tossed him away like he was nothing. He had every right to feel disappointed and that I failed him.

I pushed the comforter off me, slipped my feet into my shoes, put on some clothes, ignored the diaper that I had separated for this morning, barely remembering the fact that I had once been in a situation where I couldn't even walk.

I took another look outside, perhaps hoping that his patrol car was just going to show up at the intersection between the roads, but when I realized that that wasn't going to happen, I went outside and headed to the bus stop.

I took the bus to his house, remembering that I seldom came here when I could. Even when I couldn't walk and move my arms freely again, I refrained from coming here. It wasn't that I didn't like the place, but that I had few reasons to come here because he was always at my house.

I knocked on the door of his house, but nothing happened. I didn't hear anything coming from inside it, which was telling. That meant that he was somewhere in town and working. And given that he wasn't answering my calls, there was a nifty way to show him that I regretted everything I did and that I wasn't showing him the love he deserved.

I went to one of my friends, grabbed his massive boom boxes, put them outside in the middle of downtown, and then prepped the megaphone. I tested it to make sure that it was working, looked around me, checking out the people as they gathered around me.

It was going to be mad, but there was no way around it. Anything less than what I was doing would mean that Roderick would think that I was only trying to make myself feel less bad.

"Roderick," I said on the megaphone, sounding so loud that I was pretty sure that Roderick could hear me. The town wasn't too big and he should be somewhere in it. "I don't know where you are, but after what happened last night, I want to say that I'm sorry. I know that I treated you like trash and that there is nothing that can be done to erase that. If you hate me now, that's fine, but at least give me a chance to explain myself."

I took a second to breathe and then paused, checking the people around me. Their eyes betrayed their confusion. They had no idea what it was that was happening, but they were soon going to figure it out.

"After spending the year with you, the truth is that I love you. You are the love of my life, and I haven't forgotten that. I promised you that even after I got better, we were going to be together, and I didn't lie. I'm never going to change and I hope that you never do as well."

Everyone covered their mouths as they tried to hide their surprise, but it was pointless. I just showed everyone in town that I was in love with another guy, another man, and I was pretty sure that meant we were going to have to live elsewhere.

RODERICK'S EPILOGUE

I brushed my finger over his cheek, looking outside his bedroom while we were on his bed. It was snowing outside and the moon was high in the sky, the stars around it looking as if the world was happy now that we were together again.

I was behind him, with my arms wrapped around his body, still finding it unbelievable that he grabbed a megaphone and started telling everyone loudly in town that we were together, that he was in love with me, and that he was sorry for the way he treated me.

"I don't know what got into me, but it's over now. I guess I just got too used to the fact that you are with me and that you are always here. I was just so happy that I was doing the things I was used to doing, that my friends were coming here more often, and that everything was going back to normal. I didn't forget how important you are to me, but it stopped being new."

A tear came out of his eye, rolling down his cheek. I brushed it away with my finger and then I kissed his cheek, turning him around so that his eyes were looking at me.

I grabbed his shoulders, looking straight into his eyes as well as I said, "You did much better than Wilton after we broke up. You came back to me, told me how sorry you were about it, and even did that silly thing in front of everyone in town. They will never forget that and I also won't."

Douglas chuckled, throwing his arms around me and hugging

me tightly. I retributed the hug and then let him cry in my chest, time passing until he was better.

When he was, I kissed him again, our kiss passionate from the get-go. I even dug my tongue into his mouth, loving the way that he was battling against it until he lost control and fully gave himself to me.

We broke the kiss and then I took him to his bed, tucking ourselves under the comforter.

It was warm and the look in his eyes told me that he was most likely thinking the same thing. I got the confirmation I was looking for when I grabbed his thigh, roaming my hand on it, feeling how soft and smooth his skin was.

"Do you want to do it?" I asked, my voice like a murmur.

He nodded gently and I took off his diaper, putting it on the floor. It wasn't dirty, so he could use it again. I felt his skin with my hands, kneading it, bringing him immense pleasure, so much so that he arched his body against me, hugging me tightly again.

I then lifted my hand and wrapped my fingers around his hard-on, stroking it a couple of times until he was hard and close to orgasming. I wasn't going to give him orgasm denial like it happened that first time when he almost lost his virginity, too.

Instead, I kept on going, pumping his shaft more strongly and with a lot more vigor, until he erupted and coated my fingers with his milk. I could feel how warm and sticky it was, and the gentle look in his eyes told me that he loved that and that he wanted to do it again.

"That was amazing. You are perfect at it."

"There's much more where that came from," I said, moving on the bed until I reached out with my hand where the dresser was, opening the top drawer and grabbing something from inside it. It was a condom, which I tore open. Douglas perked up, moving so that he was standing right in front of me. I was with my knees on the bed and my hand on my dick. I was already naked even before we entered the room, knowing that this was going to happen. I always knew that we were going to make love and that I would probably take his V-card.

He grabbed the condom from my hand, putting it on me a moment later. Doug was careful and slow as he did that, his hands shaking slightly. It was almost like he knew that what he was dealing with could hurt him and, most likely, it would when I breached his asshole.

I patted him on his right asscheek, saying, "Turn around and show me your ass. You know what I want to do."

He nodded, obeying me. He parted his asscheeks slightly as he invited me in and I had no choice but to go on with it. With my cock covered and protected by the condom, I felt okay with penetrating him. I shifted on the bed so that I was in the right position, which was on top of him, and then I lined up my dick to his waiting orifice, sliding it in.

I pushed it in all the way until it was lodged inside of him, loving how warm and tight he was. I could see that he was frowning and showing pain on his face, but he didn't ask me to pull out. If anything, he was urging me to go on.

"How are you feeling right now?" I asked and when he nodded, I started to roll my hips slowly. I was doing it slowly in the beginning to lessen the pain that he felt all over his body, and I could tell that it was working.

I picked up the pace when I felt that he was more comfortable. And then, I erupted inside of him, shooting my come in my condom. I pulled out moments later and wrapped him in my arms, hugging him while he cradled his head in the crook of my neck and said over and over how sorry he was for being an ass.

I caressed the back of his head while murmuring into his ear, "It's okay. Don't worry." Minutes later, when I almost feared that he was already napping, I asked, "Do you remember my book?"

He nodded once and slowly, and then I said, "It's finished. I'll read it to you. I think that you should finally know everything about me."

And then we both fell asleep, knowing that so many things were going to change from now on. And one of them was moving out of Hope River.

The End

Leave your **review.** Your feedback is important!

TEASER: FIREFIGHTER'S PUNISHED LITTLE

ABDL MM Romance (Small Town Littles – 1)

Blake

When it came to diapers, nothing could hold me back. That was why I dissected that one diaper behind the glass panel, wishing that I was loving it with my hands. But I couldn't and the reason for that was pretty simple. Every time that I diverted my eyes down, I caught sight of the price tag, realizing that it was too high, especially for someone living in the middle of nowhere.

A small town. Hope River was the kind of place where people over 60 came to retire and I just couldn't imagine myself living here for much longer. For one, finding gay dates was pretty much impossible, not to mention the nasty repercussions that would come. People would shun me, think that I was less than human, and I didn't want that ruining my life right now more than it already was.

I wasn't going to say that I was poor to the point of not having food on the table, but it wasn't good, either. I had food. I could go to the local farmers' street market and buy whatever I wanted, but it wasn't enough. I wanted more than that. The food commercials that popped up on the news that I couldn't get my curious hands on? They allured me all the time to a life I knew I would never have.

On a side note – and a very important one at that – I couldn't show my true self to others. I was a little and always had been one. I refused to grow up and get older. People looked at me and thought that I was still underage, even though I just crossed that infamous adult-enough-to-drink line and could drink pretty much anything, not that it mattered, anyway. I didn't want to spend my nights drinking my sorrows away. That wasn't how I saw the world and I'd rather kill myself before letting something like that happen. It just would never.

The diaper that was in the store was unlike anything I'd seen in my life and it would fit me. It wasn't a diaper for babies or little boys. Rather, it was something built differently. A small town meant that most people that lived here were pretty old and Hope River wasn't any different.

I couldn't stop wanting the diaper that was in the store and I wanted to rip it out of it right away. My hands were pressing against the panel and I could feel as if I was melting into the store, ready to become one with it. But it was pretty difficult convincing myself that I could spend 5000,00 dollars on that one single diaper, especially given that it couldn't be used more than a couple of times.

That's right. The diaper was built so differently that you could wash and dry it and it would still be usable.

Not to mention the special material that it was made of, that it was supposed to be extra comfy, how it let the skin breathe, that it was supposed to make you feel like you were walking in the clouds, and all those things...

Alek

"I'm so sorry about this. I was just going there and I didn't see you until it was too late," I said, feeling very awkward about it even though I knew it was something I could fix, especially with a nice dinner made by me. I was pretty sure that the guy I was helping to get up was one of the many in town that thought I couldn't be a cook, even though I was. A long time ago, when I didn't even live in this town, I used to be a cook. I used to cook pretty much everything and anything I wanted, which was one reason why I enjoyed life so much. I wasn't going to say that it was bad, but it used to be better, though.

His eyes were shocked by what I was doing, which was nothing short of expected. After all, I wasn't just helping him up by holding him with my hand. I actually looped my arm around his torso, feeling how much smaller than me he was, not that it was something I always paid attention to whenever I was helping someone. This time, it was just something I noticed, which was weird. It was the first time I noticed that about someone.

I didn't know this guy's age, but he appeared to be young, maybe even underage. His cheeks were buttery-smooth and even though I couldn't touch them right now, I was pretty sure they were also cotton-soft. But just like it was with everyone else in this town, I shouldn't even be harboring those thoughts about him. He was probably straight and was with one of the girls that lived here.

I looked for a ring on his finger and I couldn't find any. That didn't mean he wasn't taken, but I wasn't going to give myself false hope. I kept that in mind as I pulled him up, still finding it a little funny the way he was looking at me. It was as though he was nothing more than a lost little rabbit in the woods that spotted a wolf for the first time. He was disoriented, confused, and wanted to ask me several questions.

I wasn't going to lie and say that I didn't want to stay here to answer all the questions he had for me, but I didn't have enough time for that. So much so that I had to wave my hand over my head and say, "Don't worry about me. I'm going to be with you guys soon. There's just this tiny little mistake I made and that I'm going to fix."

They were my friends, the firefighters. They were rushing over to the building where violent flames were gobbling it up. I could even see the smoke billowing up from where I was. I had no idea if the guy I helped up was aware of it, but it was possible that he wasn't. After all, he appeared to be lost in his own thoughts.

"No, it's uhh... okay. You didn't see me," he said when he realized I wasn't supporting him anymore. Not only was he very small and short, but he was also feather light. I didn't enjoy boasting about it, but I was pretty sure that I could pick him up with just one arm, which wasn't something I did every day...

OTHER MM ABDL BOOKS

SERIES - BROKEN LITTLES

1. Rockstar's Little: ABDL MM Halloween Romance
2. Doctor's Little: ABDL MM Halloween Romance
3. Biker's Little for Christmas: ABDL MM Stuck Together MC Romance
4. Rockstar's Little for Christmas: ABDL MM Secret Relationship Romance
5. Quarterback's Little: ABDL Rejected Marriage MM Romance
6. Stalker's Sweet Little: ABDL MM Romance

SERIES - REGRESSED

1. Gifting Crayons: An ABDL MM Romance
2. Sugar Mister: An ABDL MM Romance
3. Loving Little Chris: An ABDL MM Romance
4. Bedtime for Cody: An ABDL MM Romance
5. Little Crayons: An ABDL MM Romance

ABOUT THE AUTHOR

Jerry Hastings biggest love? Writing MM ABDL books. He can't go a day without imagining worlds where littles find their Daddies and live their HEAs. His stories are peppered with diapers, pacis, and coloring books.

His best-sellers are 'Quarterback's Little' and 'My Caring Biker', which are books that he'll always remember fondly. Check them out on his author page if you are interested.

www.ingramcontent.com/pod-product-compliance
Lightning Source LLC
Chambersburg PA
CBHW052116150726
48002CB00006B/2375